The Devouring
F.W. Armstrong

A TOM DOHERTY ASSOCIATES BOOK

This is a work of fiction. All the characters and events portrayed in this book are fictional, and any resemblance to real people or incidents is purely coincidental.

THE DEVOURING

Copyright © 1987 by F.W. Armstrong

All rights reserved, including the right to reproduce this book or portions thereof in any form.

First printing: April 1987

A TOR Book

Published by Tom Doherty Associates, Inc.
49 West 24 Street
New York, N.Y. 10010

ISBN: 0-812-52758-5
CAN. ED.: 0-812-52759-3

Printed in the United States of America

0 9 8 7 6 5 4 3 2 1

THE FIRST VICTIMS

The woman's head was buried in the left side of Vera's neck. Only her arms and the upper part of her head and face were visible, because Vera's quivering body blocked the rest of her.

For a moment John resented Vera for blocking his view of the woman's incredible body. He said, "Vera?" and wanted to add, *Get out of the way*, but realized that he couldn't say that to her, that they'd shared twenty-seven years and had produced six children and now her life was coming to an end—it was obvious; the red stain on the back of her housedress was growing larger by the second.

Vera's body shook violently, and she fell with a massive thump to the hardwood floor.

The woman standing over her turned her gaze on John. He stared at her perfect nakedness, then into her eyes as she swept toward him. And he was as pleased and eager as an infant at its mother's breast to make himself her next victim.

The Devouring

Tor books by F.W. Armstrong

**THE CHANGING
THE DEVOURING**

*To Miles Wright,
who died August 29, 1986*

*And to Victor,
without whom this book would have been
much much harder to write*

Part One

Item from the *Buffalo Evening News*

October 15

TRANSIENT FOUND DEAD

The body of Wilson Goode, 56, no known address, was found by sanitation workers in a dumpster on Lawrence Street, at the heart of what is commonly known as "The District," Friday morning. According to Buffalo's 10th Precinct Captain, Jack Lucas, Goode had apparently been dead for several days. Chief Lucas could not disclose the cause of death, saying only, "It is under investigation. We do not at this point suspect foul play."

Goode's last known address, according to people in the area, was the Peacock Hotel, on Gadow Street. There are no known survivors.

Chapter One

In Buffalo, New York

"How many is that, Vera?" John asked from his La-Z-Boy.

"Twenty-two," Vera answered. Vera—a chunky forty-five—kept track of trick-or-treaters. The previous Halloween there had been forty-seven of them, five more than the year before, but three less than the year before that. "Eight Frankensteins, two ghosts," she went on; she also kept track of costumes—keeping track of things was an obsession with her. She kept track of birthday cards, sunny days, gray squirrels (there were thirty-one of them, she insisted, in the twin maple trees in front of the house), salesmen, robins; anything that could repeat itself and therefore could be kept track of, she kept track of with a vengeance. She continued her litany of trick-or-treaters: "Three skeletons, one gremlin—"

The Devouring

"A Gremlin?" her husband John cut in. "Someone came dressed as a car?"

"A car?"

"Sure." He was making a small joke. He knew well enough what Gremlins were; he'd taken their five-year-old granddaughter, Amy, to see the movie. "A Gremlin; AMC makes them."

"AMC?" Vera asked, confused.

John sighed; *Another gem down the toilet*, he thought. "Forget it," he said.

She went on. "And six witches, one werewolf, two vampires—" She stopped; someone had knocked at the door. "And there's another one," she said. She went to the door, put her hand on the knob, glanced critically at the two large wooden bowls—one stocked with small packets of M&Ms, the other with candied apples—on a table to the right of the doorway. She'd have to restock soon, she thought. She opened the door.

"Trick or treat!" the five kids standing on the porch screamed in unison. Vera quickly surveyed their costumes—two witches (witches were popular this year), something that looked like a dog, a Ronald Reagan—a costume she disapproved of because it showed flagrant disrespect—and another skeleton, though the little girl wearing that costume had taken the skeleton hood off, probably to give herself some breathing room this warm Halloween night.

"You're all *very* scary!" Vera shivered, and

as she shivered her body vibrated beneath her flower print housedress.

"Trick or treat!" the kids screamed again, except for the pretty brown-haired, green-eyed girl in the skeleton costume, who looked vaguely pouty and put out, as if Vera were wasting her time.

Vera said to her, concerned, "Are you having a good time, honey?"

The girl nodded once glumly.

From inside the Ronald Reagan costume the voice of a small boy chirped, "Trick or treat!" as if to hurry things along.

"Just a moment," Vera said firmly but gently, and looked around at the two bowls on the table behind the door. She looked back at the trick-or-treaters. "Let me see," she began. "How many—" She stopped. The pretty girl in the skeleton costume was gone. Vera stepped forward and leaned with her hands on the door frame. She looked left down the row of well-lighted lawns and then right, down a row of equally well-lighted lawns; a number of other trick-or-treaters were going to and coming from the neat two-story houses that made up Hydrangea Avenue. In the roadway some cars were stopped and some were moving very slowly, all of them, Vera supposed, driven by the parents of trick-or-treaters. But she saw no pretty brown-haired girl in a skeleton costume, so she shrugged and got down to the business of handing out candied apples and M&Ms to the kids who remained.

An hour later John got wearily up from his La-Z-Boy and trundled into the kitchen for a snack. His habit was always to snack before retiring anyway; usually something heavy, something loaded with salt and laced with cholesterol—a ham sandwich with mayonnaise, mustard, and Colby cheese on deli rye, for instance, with a big glass of ice cold milk on the side. That's what he thought he'd like tonight.

He opened the refrigerator door and peered in glumly. "Vera?" he called. Vera was in the living room, in her own chair, a three-quarter-size pale violet upholstered version of John's dark green leatherette La-Z-Boy. She was knitting a bulky red sweater, probably, she thought, for John. She'd decide for certain when it was almost finished. If it was too small, it would go to her nephew, Floyd. If it was too large—which seemed unlikely—she'd put it in the Salvation Army bin.

"Yes, John?" she called back.

"I thought we had ham, Vera. Where's the ham?"

Before Vera could answer, there was a soft knock at the door. She got up, sighing. On her way to answer the knock, she stuck her head into the kitchen doorway. "I used it in the soup this afternoon," she said.

"Soup?" John said. "I didn't see any soup."

"I froze it," Vera explained.

Another soft knock. John glanced in the direction of the front door. "What's that? Some more trick-or-treaters? God almighty, it's"—he checked the teapot-shaped kitchen clock over the sink—"it's almost ten o'clock."

"Last year," Vera said, rummaging about in her memory, "they kept coming until eleven-fifteen."

John shook his head. There was another soft knock at the front door—no more urgent, no louder, and so, in its repetitive way, very insistent. "What kind of parent would let their kid trick-or-treat till ten o'clock at night, Vera?"

She said, "I don't know, John," and went to answer the door while John poked gloomily about in the refrigerator.

Before Vera put her hand on the doorknob, there was another knock; it was the same as the first three—a soft triple knock, the knock of a child, she thought. But she hesitated. She hesitated because she sensed danger. Vera had a sixth sense about such things. She had stopped counting the number of times, for instance, that she'd hesitated over a chicken leg or a forkful of fish because she was certain that an errant bone waited to strangle the life out of her, and, upon investigation, usually found that she was right.

"Yes?" she called now through the front door.

Her only answer was yet another soft triple knock.

John called from the kitchen, "Hey, this mayonnaise is rancid, for chrissake!"

"That's yogurt," she called back. "Florence made it." Florence was Vera's best friend.

"Yogurt?!" John called, as if the word itself smelled bad.

Another soft triple knock sounded from the front door.

Vera sighed quickly, with agitation. She wished she were tall enough to peer through the two small rectangular windows in the top of the door. She stared fixedly at the door itself, as if conjuring up the ability to see through it. "Damn!" she breathed; she'd have to ask John to look into installing one of those security peepholes in the center of the door.

John called, "Well, *I'm* not going to eat it!"

And Vera, sighing, pulled the front door open.

The pretty brown-haired girl in the skeleton costume, *sans* hood, smiled appealingly up at her. "Hello, Mrs. Brownleigh," she said.

Vera's smile, which had appeared automatically, vanished. "How do you know our name?" she asked, although the literal answer was obvious; *The Brownleighs* was emblazoned in stylized black letters just to the right of the front door. What she had meant to ask, but hadn't had the time to figure out how to phrase, was, *Why do you greet me as if you've known me all your life?* She was, in fact, starting to construct just such a sentence when the pretty brown-haired girl on her doorstep began to change.

She got taller, first, though her face remained that of a thirteen- or fourteen-year-old. Rapidly, and fluidly, as if enacting a precise time lapse of the next decade of her life, she grew a good ten inches. And her body matured, too, her hips flared and her breasts blossomed, and the skeleton costume, which did not change, shredded down the sides and held precariously at the left shoulder.

A quivering, incredulous smile appeared on Vera's mouth. "Are you all right, honey?" she whispered raggedly, as if the girl had merely put her hand to her stomach, or had looked suddenly pale, or had asked for a glass of water. Because, very simply, how could she—Vera—actually be seeing what she thought she was seeing? Clearly something was wrong here, but just as clearly it was something wrong with her, with Vera, as much as with the pretty brown-haired girl. Clearly the sun did not rise in the west, and if, one morning, it appeared to, then someone was simply mistaken about directions.

The change hesitated there—the playfully grinning thirteen- or fourteen-year-old face on the electrifyingly sensuous body of a twenty-year-old woman.

That's when John appeared from the kitchen. He had a bottle of Coke in one hand, a cheese sandwich in the other, and when he saw what Vera was seeing, a huge and lustful grin played on his mouth momentarily. Until he realized that what he was looking at was not quite right somehow, that it was even a little obscene—like goats surgically altered to look like unicorns. That sweet and pretty little girl's face had no business there, on that incredible body.

"Vera?" he managed. "Who's that?"

Vera shook her head slowly. She said nothing.

The skeleton costume fell, revealing the nakedness beneath.

And the change resumed. The eyes lost their innocence, the playful grin became a sneer. And the mouth opened very, very wide, the way a snake's mouth opens to take in the body of a mouse.

John dropped his bottle of Coke. It thudded to the floor, bounced on the hard wood; the lip of the bottle hit his ankle and he glanced at it, muttered a small, confused *Urp!* of pain, looked back at the woman in the doorway.

Her head was buried in the left side of Vera's neck. Only her arms, the top of her head, something of her forehead, and the bridge of her nose were visible because Vera's quivering body in the flower print housedress blocked the rest of her.

And for a moment John resented Vera for that. For blocking his view of the woman's incredible body. He smiled in anticipation. He said, "Vera?" and wanted to add, *Get out of the way*, but realized he couldn't say that to her, that she was still his wife; they'd shared twenty-seven years and had produced six children and now that her life was coming to an end—it was obvious; the red stain on the back of her housedress was growing larger by the second—he had to say something comforting to her, something to sum up their lives together, something short and simple and sweet, something that would surely push through the shock and fear that had to be consuming her—just as that incredible body was consuming her—and into her heart.

"Vera," he said, "you really knew how to keep track of things."

Vera's body quivered violently, and she fell with a massive thump to the hardwood floor.

Then the woman standing over her turned her gaze on John. And he turned his gaze on her—on her nakedness, first. Then on her eyes as she swept toward him. And he was as pleased and as eager as an infant at its mother's breast to make himself her next victim.

* * *

In another part of Buffalo, where the rats outnumbered the humans a hundred to one, a woman pushed open the door of a seedy bar, moved fetchingly over to a table, and sat down. The night was unseasonably warm, and she was in a voluptuous, low-cut, tight green dress and high heels.

At the other end of the bar, one of two men sitting playing poker nudged his buddy—who had his back turned to the woman—and said loudly enough that he hoped the woman could hear him, "Looka that, Sam. I wouldn't mind givin' *her* a poke or two."

Sam glanced around and saw the woman; his face broke into a broad, sleazy grin. "What's she doin' in here, I wonder, Hap?"

Hap said, "Only one way to find out," and he stood and made his way over to the woman.

She didn't acknowledge him at once, so he said, "How you doin', honey?"

She glanced slowly up at him. A chill coursed through him. He'd never seen eyes like hers before—they were huge, and brown and beautiful and . . . distant. As if, as she looked at him, her eyes were on something else entirely. And her little flat grin, Hap thought, was like the one that Sam got when they watched porno flicks together.

He pressed on. "My name's Hap. What's yours?"

The bartender, a beefy guy in his early forties who'd spent several years as a professional wrestler, bellowed, "What'll it be, lady?"

Her gaze turned slowly from Hap to the bartender. "Sloe gin fizz," she said, and her gaze drifted back to Hap. Another chill went through him. He nodded. "Nice meetin' you, huh?" he said, and hurried back to his table.

"Not my type," he said sullenly to his friend Sam, and sat down.

Sam took a long, appreciative look at the woman. "Well, she's sure as hell mine," he said.

Six Months Earlier

In a little town twenty miles south of the Pennsylvania border, near Erie, a middle-aged man and woman laid a wreath on the grave of their teenage daughter, Lila, dead exactly two months. The man, whose name was Will Curtis, was wearing a heavy gray coat to protect himself from the mid-April chill and supported himself with a cane because of arthritis. He nodded sullenly at the grave and said to the woman, his voice slight and creaking, "All her life she was a good girl, Frances. She was a nice girl. She ran away, but she came back to us. She was a nice girl."

But Frances said nothing. Frances believed otherwise. She let her husband rattle on: "It's impossible . . . it's impossible to protect ourselves totally from the . . . evils . . ." He fought back a tear; it returned and slid down his weathered cheek. He finished, ". . . the evils of this world, Frances."

She nodded. "Yes," she said. She knew it was the truth.

He took her hand and said again, "The evils of this world." He thought a moment. "The evils of this *fucking* world!"

"Yes," Frances said.

"I'm sorry," he said.

"For what?"

"For using the 'F' word here. In front of Lila."

She squeezed his hand. "It doesn't matter. She hears no words at all." And that, Frances thought, surely was the truth—thank God, it surely was the truth.

Chapter Two

In Boston

"Yes, Coreen," sighed Ryerson Biergarten, "I realize that I look like a slob. And no, I don't *like* to look like a slob, and I really would do something about it if I—"

His first wife, who went these days by the name of Coreen Savage, sneered and cut in. "If you *wanted* to, Doctor." She called him "doctor" now as a kind of prod. When they were married, she called him doctor because he held a doctorate in parapsychology from Duke University, and although no one else called him doctor, because he didn't encourage it, for her, he knew, it had been a title filled with implied status and self-serving pride. Ryerson Biergarten knew many things, not only through the normal processes of education and living, but also because he was an astoundingly gifted psychic. His casual handsomeness and his unparalleled work as a psychic investigator had made him the darling of the popular press, and although he claimed to dislike the popular press, he'd admitted grudgingly that when *People* magazine had featured him on its cover ten months earlier, it had made him feel very good.

Ryerson—his friends called him Rye—also was a man who made mistakes, a fact with which he would have quickly agreed, and one of his choicest mistakes, he maintained, was marrying Coreen. "The old, old story," he said once, "of the triumph of biology over good sense."

"And what," Coreen whined on, "are you doing with that dis*gusting* dog?"

"I like him," Ryerson protested.

"Well, for heaven's sake, he *sounds* like he's going to die!"

Ryerson shook his head. "No," he said, and stroked his Boston bull terrier pup, Creosote—so named because Ryerson had found him, shivering and thin and just a lick away from death, six months earlier in a smokehouse in Massachusetts. "He's not going to die, Coreen. He's got asthma. It's a fault of the breed—"

"Breed?" Coreen said incredulously. "Breed, Doctor? Are you saying that that *dog* has a *ped*igree?"

Coreen was the quintessential bitch. She was also a knockout. She was tall, buxom, red-haired; she had a small, pouty mouth, huge bright-green eyes, and she possessed the sort of natural sensuality that made *everyone* turn around and look. She used this sensuality to her best advantage. No one could blame her, least of all Ryerson, who, fifteen years earlier, had been one of its first wide-eyed and willing victims.

He said now, "Did you get the part you were after, Coreen?"

And she answered, from the small gray love seat in Ryerson's Newbury Street row house, "Which one?"

He smiled wearily. Was *Which one?* merely a pose—*Well, you know, Rye, there are literally dozens of producers after me.* He could not easily peer into her psyche for the answer. He had never been able to peer easily into her psyche. It was like looking into the head of a wild animal; what he saw was usually a mass of harsh angles and static and snow— it was, in fact, one of the things that he found attractive about her in the first place, beyond her obvious physical attributes. It made her mysterious, unreachable, and thus, at the time—when he was still working toward his doctorate at Duke University—a challenge.

He had quickly found that if he could not easily peer into her mind, it was, sadly, because there was precious little to see. Her concerns in life were basic—food, control, sex, sleep, comfort, and status. The order of those concerns varied from day to day and week to week, of course, as they do with everyone, but control always stayed near the top of the list.

She exercised control, of course, with her body and her sensuality. She controlled Ryerson for the three years of their stormy marriage because she got a kick out of controlling him, and Ryerson let himself be controlled because, of course, he loved going to bed with her. It was a pit that he was not about to let himself fall into twelve years later, as she sat prettily on the small love seat, clearly offering herself to him in return for some as yet unasked for favor.

She sighed and let a sad little grin play on her mouth. "Well, actually, Rye"—Ryerson stiffened; she never called him Rye—"I didn't get the part I was after." She'd been auditioning for a part in a big-budget horror movie called *Strange Seed*, which was to be shot near Boston. She'd charmed the director, the associate director, the assistant director, a few of the camera operators, and even the male secretary to the producer; the part, she felt certain, was hers. She had failed, however, to consider that the world she moved in turned not on sex alone or on money alone, but on sex and money together, and, bedroom favors aside, there were other women better for the part. She added, "Someone else got it. Someone named *Irene!*" She said the name as if it were a forkful of bad fish she was trying to get out of her mouth.

"My sister's name is Irene," Ryerson said, smiling to himself.

"And she has a face like an owl," Coreen said.

"My sister has a face like an owl?" Ryerson said. "No, she doesn't."

Coreen waved the observation away. "No, not your sister. This person who got *my* part. She has a face like an owl, like one of those white owls you see on cigar boxes—"

"A barn owl?" Ryerson observed. He stroked Creosote, who gurgled, grunted, and licked happily at Ryerson's chin. "What's the part?"

"The part?" Coreen asked, momentarily confused—which was nothing new—then hurried on. "Oh, the part. Yes. It was the part of a dead woman. Some woman who died and came back to life."

Ryerson shrugged. "Well, it seems ready-made for someone who looks like an owl."

Coreen looked at him. "Is that a joke?"

Ryerson smiled thinly. "Sort of, Coreen." He paused. "Listen, I'm sorry, but if you've come here for a favor—"

She cut in sharply, as if offended. "A favor? My God, Rye, husbands and wives don't do *favors* for each other. What*ever* they do, they do out of love." She gave him a straight and serious look, as if she had just uttered an astounding profundity. Then she smiled coyly. "And since you are, as they say, not without influence—"

"First of all, we aren't husband and wife anymore, thank the good Lord, and secondly, yes—I am completely without influence. I wouldn't *want* to influence anyone, Coreen, even if I could . . ."

"All I'm saying is that you know people. And because you know people—"

"No," Ryerson said firmly.

She looked appraisingly up at him from the love seat for a half minute, trying to gauge the firmness of his position. Then, nodding slowly, she went on, "Yes, of course. I understand. But you know, Rye, what makes this world go around—"

"No," he said again.

"Well then, I'll tell you," she said, misinterpreting his answer.

"No," he said yet again, very firmly. "You're not going to tell me what makes the world go around. I *know* what makes the world go around. Inertia. Not sex or money or whatever it is you were going to say, Coreen. Inertia! Conservation of momentum! We learned about it in high school."

She sighed heavily, in resignation, and stood. She was normally almost as tall as Ryerson; now, wearing very high heels, she contrived to appear even taller. She conjured up her most regal and offended look—chin jutting forward, eyes looking at Ryerson down the bridge of her nose, and she said, "You are *weird*, Doctor." It was a phrase she had used quite a lot during the breakup of their marriage and Ryerson said now, as he had so often then, "No more than anyone else, Coreen."

She focused on Creosote, who was trying mightily to lick Ryerson's chin. "And so," she finished, "is your disgusting dog!" Then she stomped from the house.

Joan Mott Evans had never been in Boston before and she wasn't sure what she thought of it. She found the Boston accent intriguing, and the people passably friendly, at least the few she'd met—a bus driver, a drugstore clerk, a cop who'd given her directions to Newbury Street. But the aura of the city seemed stiffer than she was used to. She'd lived in Buffalo for the past several months, but she thought of Erie, Pennsylvania, as her real home, and before that, Brockport, New York, home of Brockport State College. She was used to small towns and small concerns, where it was true that everyone knew everyone else's business, but it was also true that if you were in trouble, a lot of people knew about it, and someone was usually willing to help.

Boston wasn't at all like that. How could it be? Crowds made people turn inward, and look for identity within themselves; crowds made people yearn to be something other than just another face, or another body. And what was a city like Boston if not simply a very well-mannered crowd? She grinned self-critically. Or maybe, she decided, she was reading much more into what the city was telling her than she ought to; maybe she wasn't being fair.

She turned her head to look at the number of the row house to her right. "Damn," she whispered, because, as usual, caught up in her thoughts, she'd lost track of where she was and what she was doing. Ryerson Biergarten—whom she'd come from Buffalo to see—lived at a number behind her and on the other side of the street. She pulled his letter from the pocket of her simple rust-colored fall jacket and checked the return address. She repocketed the letter, and, not for the first time, had misgivings about being here, in Boston, on her way to see the most celebrated and successful of the nation's psychics. She thought, also not for the first time, that it was like the criminal hanging around the police station and acting nervous. Sooner or later someone was bound to ask questions, and sooner or later all the terrible answers would come spilling out. Especially if the someone asking the questions was Ryerson H. Biergarten.

She turned around, started back down Newbury Street. She saw Ryerson's house almost at once. It was a two-story white row house with black shutters on long, narrow windows. And there was a tall, attractive woman coming out the front door. Joan caught the woman's eye and the name "Coreen" flashed through her head. *Doesn't fit her*, Joan thought. *She looks like a bitch.* But the name, she realized, could have come from anywhere. It could have come from some elderly man sitting in one of the row houses, for instance, his thoughts on a long-dead love affair. That sort of thing had happened before, as if the frequency of Joan's psychic receiver changed at random, so, from time to time, what she received was a burst of something totally unrelated to the moment. She had a quick and urgent desire to call out the name, to see how the woman would react, but within a few moments the woman climbed into a late model LTD Crown Victoria and was speeding away from her, southwest down Newbury Street. Joan sighed; these quick bursts of psychic input were always strangely wearying.

A few moments later she was ringing Ryerson Biergarten's doorbell.

Chapter Three

In Buffalo, New York

Laurie Drake said to her best friend Jennifer Wright, "They do too eat people."

Jennifer rolled her eyes. "No, no, no, Laurie—*werewolves* eat people."

They were coming out of an advanced placement class in mythology at the Henrietta Heberling Memorial Junior-Senior High School and were on their way to lunch. They were best friends because most of the other kids in the school thought they were strange and unapproachable. The fact was that they were very bright, brighter in fact by half than their classmates, and so they had gravitated to each other. Jennifer, however, couldn't help but think that Laurie could be impossibly dense at times. She went on, her tone very instructional. "Vampires are subtle, Laurie. They feed, but they don't feed too much. They don't waste anything."

Laurie would hear none of it. "I know what I saw—"

Jennifer cut in, laughing, "My God, it was only a movie."

"Nothing is *only* anything, Jennifer," Laurie interrupted icily. "Don't you think that people *research* these things?! Of course they do. Besides, what we're talking about here is *hunger*! Have you ever been hungry, Jennifer?" She paused; they both knew the answer to that—Jennifer had never wanted for anything. Laurie nodded sagely. "Of course you haven't. *I* have. I've been hungry enough to eat an old shoe—and let me tell you something—"

Behind them a man's voice said, "Hurry along, girls." They turned their heads in unison to see the physical education teacher, Mr. Piper, behind them. He added, "Cheeseburgers today; you don't want to miss out on cheeseburgers, do you?" And he slid gracefully past them and into the cafeteria. "What a fox!" Jennifer whispered.

Laurie would normally have agreed very heartily, but her stomach—which had been aching on and off now for several days—suddenly began to ache very badly, so her only response was a whispered "Uh-huh."

In Boston

Hell, Ryerson thought, convinced that Coreen had returned for another whack at him.

The Devouring

"No!" he called, although he was on the second floor of the house and whoever was ringing the doorbell couldn't possibly hear him. With Creosote in his arms, he made his way down the open spiral staircase to the front door. He hesitated. The doorbell rang again. He looked down at Creosote, whose tongue was wagging at him. "It's a woman, isn't it, boy?" Creosote's tongue wagged harder. Ryerson went on. "And it's not Coreen, is it?" Creosote's tongue disappeared into his mouth; he cocked his head questioningly. "It's a stranger," Ryerson said. "Someone from out-of-state." Creosote's head cocked to the other direction; his tongue reappeared briefly.

Ryerson pulled the door open.

He had never seen Joan Mott Evans before. He had tracked her down to Buffalo, using various standard sources—the Census Bureau, the Bureau of Vital Statistics, the New York Motor Vehicle Department. At the beginning he had only her first name to go on, which was given to him by the parents of poor, damned Lila Curtis; "Our daughter had a friend," Mrs. Curtis had told him. "Someone she confided in, someone she looked up to, like a big sister. She said her name was Joan." He had a good description of her, too, also given to him by Lila's parents. And eventually, using those two pieces of information—Joan's first name and her description—it had been easy enough to track her down, although when he'd arrived at her house in Buffalo two months earlier, there had been no answer to his knock.

"Yes?" he said now.

"Hi," said Joan Mott Evans with a slight, unconvincing smile, as if sorry she were disturbing him. "We've never met, Mr. Biergarten." Her smile flattened. "Not formally, anyway."

"Yes?" he said again.

"I was in the city visiting a friend—her name's Nadine Homer; perhaps you know her."

Ryerson shook his head. "No, I'm afraid not." The description that Lila Curtis's parents had given him had been very accurate—short auburn hair, a round, appealing face, small straight nose, large, round, expressive gray eyes; "She's very nice to look at," Lila's father had said. "She's no beauty queen, but she *is* nice to look at."

Mrs. Curtis had merely shrugged and said, "Yes, I suppose so." She had a trim and athletic-looking body, too; Ryerson got a quick mental picture of her doing an hour's worth of aerobic exercises each morning—it was an image he liked, because he had always been a firm believer in a healthy body being necessary to the maintenance of a strong and healthy mind.

Joan rattled on, clearly nervous now, but trying hard not to show it. "I have a copy of your book. . . ." She produced a copy of

Conversations with Charlene from her purse and thrust it at him. "And I was wondering if you could autograph it for me."

He smiled graciously, took the book from her, patted the pocket of his shirt—beneath his ragged white pullover sweater—and said, "I'm sorry, I don't have a pen."

She smiled back, searched a few moments in her purse, came up with a gold Cross pen, and handed it to him. She said, as he wrote on the title page of the book, "Actually, we have met, in a way. You came to my house a month ago."

He handed her the book. "Thanks," she said, and began to stuff it into her purse.

"No," he said, "please. Read the inscription."

She smiled nervously at him. "The inscription?"

"Yes. Please read it."

She took the book from her purse, opened to the copyright page, then to the title page. She read:

> To Joan Mott Evans,
>   Let's talk.
>   Rye.

She kept her head down for a good half minute, as if reading the short inscription all that time. Then, sighing, she looked up at him. "I'm sorry," she said.

Ryerson, seeing her embarrassment, extended his arm welcomingly. "No," he said,

"I'm sorry. That was unfair. Please, come inside. I'm sure there's a lot we have to say to each other."

In Buffalo

Irene Sabitch scowled at her computer monitor in the Buffalo Police Department Records Division. Her coworker, Glen Coffman, sitting behind his own computer monitor a few feet away, said, "You look like you just chomped down on a clove of garlic, Irene. What's the problem?"

She glanced at him, still scowling, then looked back at her monitor. She said tightly, "The problem is this new system." She guffawed. "Foolproof, my ass!"

Glen got up, went over, stood behind her, and scanned her monitor. "Just punch in the user number, Irene. It's 001.BPD," and he started for his seat.

"I tried that," she said.

He stopped, looked back, shrugged. "Try it again."

"I tried it *six times*, Glen."

He went back and put his hand on her shoulder to coax her from her chair. "Let me give it a try, okay?"

She stayed put. "For God's sake, Glen, I can punch in user numbers just as well as you can."

He hesitated, looked at the screen again. He was reading the computer's "file directory."

It showed him a list of files on that particular computer disk which were available for inspection by the computer operator. It read:

FILE DIRECTORY

CURTIS L.BAK   JME.BAK   HAWKINS.LET   LET.BAK
FORMAT.CMD   STAT.CMD   OPER.CMD   JME.OPE
USER NUMBER?

He reached over Irene's shoulder and punched in "001.BPD." The screen cleared. A moment later these words appeared on it:

INVALID USER NUMBER.
RETURNING TO FILE DIRECTORY

He scowled. The file directory and its maddening "user number?" request came back on the screen. He said, "Well, someone's screwed up royally here. That user number is locked into the system—"

"I *know* that, Glen," Irene said, and glanced around at him. "You don't have to shout."

He looked back at her. "Was I shouting? I'm sorry." He studied the screen. "Where'd you get this disk?"

"From the hard disk subsystem. I was updating files, this appeared, and I made a copy of it."

"Uh-huh. That explains it then. Those files"—he nodded at the screen—"were in the system before it was restructured. So it's got a personal user number on it."

"Oh, yeah?" Irene teased. "Whose?"

"Whose?" Glen said. "I don't know. We

should have a list of personal user numbers around here somewhere. Find it and input every one till this damned file opens up."

She rolled her eyes. "Glen, do you know how many user numbers that could be?"

"Not many. A few thousand. But, hell, you type pretty fast." He chuckled, went back to his own monitor, sat down, looked back. "Hey, have you seen my games disk? I was halfway through *Space Wars* yesterday."

Lilian Janus

At thirty-three, Lilian Janus had what she considered a more or less perfect life. Her home was comfortable, she kept it neat; her children were nicely behaved and did well in school; her husband, Frank, was handsome and a good provider.

She had a part-time job as a cosmetics salesperson at Sibley's Department Store, in Buffalo. She liked the job because it enabled her to meet women she felt were much like herself, women whose only real concerns in life had to do with the inexorable approach of middle age, and, she assumed, the bothersome and sometimes unreasonable sexual overtures of their husbands. Because (everyone knew it) sex, or the promise of it, was merely something "that enables a woman to catch a husband and keeps a husband at home." Her mother, rest her sainted soul, had drilled it into her since she was twelve years old.

Chapter Four

In Boston

"I like your dog," Joan said. Ryerson had brought her a cup of coffee and some of his homemade brown Betty. She had never had brown Betty before but had developed an instant passion for it. "He's just a pup, right?"

Ryerson, looking like a proud father, said, "Yes, he is. Six months old. He's a Boston bull terrier, you know."

Joan, seated in the same gray love seat that Coreen had used, nodded. "I had one when I was a kid. My brothers hated him, but I think I was just perverse enough to really appreciate him." She stopped suddenly, thought about what she'd said, and hurried on. "I'm sorry, I didn't mean to imply—"

Ryerson, shaking his head, said, "No, please, don't apologize. I know exactly what you mean; they're like ... fruitcakes, aren't they? Everyone says you're supposed to hate them, but I don't."

Joan smiled slightly and inclined her head in acknowledgment; actually, she hated fruitcake. "Yes," she said, "I know what you're talking about." She realized then that during the ten minutes or so she'd been in his apartment her anxiety had vanished because he was so easy to be with. So far, they'd talked primarily about the city, and it was clear that he felt the same kind of paternal love and pride for it that he felt for Creosote. She liked that feeling of paternalism she saw in him. She knew that it was not the overbearing, domineering kind of paternalism that so many men harbored, but more a sort of protective affection and understanding. And when she had gotten glimpses into his psyche, she'd seen that although he was now a stable and happy man, he'd had a very troubled past. She wanted to peer at some of those troubles, but when she tried, it was like looking through ten feet of clear lake water at a half-dozen dark, amorphous shapes swimming about.

He hadn't yet asked her the reason for her visit, not, she thought, because he was baiting her with friendliness, waiting to spring it on her—to surprise some sort of confession out of her—but because he genuinely wanted to get to know her a little better.

So she was at ease when he asked, "Can

you tell me about Lila?" He was sitting in a big brown wing chair facing her at the other side of the small, cluttered room. Books composed most of the clutter. There were also loose manuscript pages here and there around his huge rolltop desk, various doggy chew toys scattered about, most of them in perfect condition, because Creosote's favorite chew toys were Ryerson's argyle socks. And there was a raft of unopened mail on a small cherry table near the door. Ryerson had Creosote in his arms, and his legs loosely crossed. He put Creosote on the floor, leaned forward, and added, "Were you and Lila friends?"

Joan answered at once, nodding vigorously, "Yes, we were friends. We were the best of friends, Rye." The name flowed freely from her lips, as if she had been calling him "Rye" for years. ("Mr. Biergarten," he'd told her, "kind of stumbles around in the mouth, doesn't it? And Ryerson doesn't fit me at all, I hope. So please call me Rye.") Joan went on, sighing first, happy to be on the verge of letting some of her awful secret out at last. "She was like a sister to me. A little sister." She leaned over, picked her coffee cup up from the hardwood floor—there were no tables near the love seat, and she'd noticed, anyway, a profusion of condensation rings on the floor from other cups—sipped the coffee, set the cup on the floor again, continued. "We were not nearly the same age, as you know. She was sixteen. I'm twenty-three. So I guess you could call it a big sister/little sister relationship."

Ryerson cut in gently, "It was nothing more than that, Joan?"

If anyone else had asked such a question, she'd have stalked from the room. But she knew that no one else could have glimpsed in her past those few hours during her sophomore year in college when she'd given herself over to what had seemed like real and honest impulses. But when those few hours were done, she had realized that although those impulses had indeed been real, and probably still were, the act itself had all but sickened her. And that was a fact she couldn't dodge. A fact she was still grappling with. She said to Ryerson, "I loved Lila. She was my friend, my confidante, and I was *her* friend and confidante. It went no further. It couldn't have."

To which Ryerson replied, "I'm sorry. I had to ask. I won't mention it again."

Joan hurried on. "When she died, I didn't know what to do. She wasn't my only friend, of course. I have friends; both men and women. People I go out with. But none of those friendships are like what I had with Lila. What I had with Lila was a once-in-a-lifetime sort of thing." Her voice was trembling now. "The sort of thing that friendships are supposed to be, I guess. Like the friendships a lot of people have only with their pets."

She stopped, looked at Creosote, then at Ryerson, went on. "I'm sorry, I didn't mean—"

Ryerson said, "Pardon me, Joan, but you seem to apologize a lot more than you need to."

She grinned wryly. "You're right. It's just that I run off at the mouth from time to time." She realized that anxiety was creeping up on her again because she was on the brink of saying more, much more, than she wanted to. And on top of it all, she had little idea how much Ryerson knew. She went on. "Just how psychic are you, Rye?"

"Very," he answered simply. It was the first bit of cat and mouse he'd played with her, she thought. He added, "And you?"

"And me what?" She sounded surprised.

He said, settling back and crossing his legs again, "I'd say you have the gift, Joan."

She opened her mouth, closed it. Then, just as he was about to speak, she blurted out, "It's not a gift, dammit! How can you call it a *gift*? It's a disease, it's a damned disease—" She stopped, shook her head, sighed heavily, and reiterated, forcing steadiness into her voice, "It's not a gift, Rye. It's *not* a gift!"

He stared silently at her for several seconds. Then he said, "Why did Lila kill herself?"

She said nothing.

"Were you there with her," Ryerson said, "when she—"

Joan cut in, "I was wrong about you."

Ryerson said nothing.

Joan added, "I thought you were going to play fair. But you're not playing fair. You're setting me up, dammit, and I don't like it." She paused to give him a chance to respond. Still he said nothing. She went on tightly. "I told myself, 'Now, here's a man who's easy to be with. Here's a man who's not going to try to dominate me, who's not going to try to trick me.' But it was all an act, wasn't it?" Still he said nothing. "*Wasn't* it?!" she demanded.

"Yes," he said. "I'm sorry."

She pushed herself quickly to her feet. "Where'd you put my jacket, dammit!"

He stood. Creosote reappeared from the bedroom with a well-chewed argyle sock hanging from his mouth. Ryerson glanced at the dog, then looked apologetically at Joan. "Please, don't leave. No more tricks, I promise. But please, don't leave. We've got to talk."

She looked fixedly at him. "It's too late, *Mr.* Biergarten. Much too late!"

"It's never too late to talk, Joan."

"And what's that? Profound utterance of the hour?" She glanced quickly about. "*Where* is my damned jacket?!"

Ryerson sighed. "I'll get it," he said, and went into the bedroom; he'd put her jacket on the bed. But when he went into the bedroom, he stopped and whispered, "Creosote, you little—"

The jacket was in shreds.

He sensed Joan behind him, turned his head, and again looked apologetically at her. He said lamely, "He likes people's clothes, I'm afraid."

Joan said nothing. She moved stiffly past him to the bed, picked up what was left of her jacket, and stalked from the room. Ryerson followed her downstairs to the front door. When she was about to open it, he said, "Where are you staying in Boston?"

She pursed her lips. "Do I have to tell you?"

He shook his head quickly. "No," he said, "you don't."

In Buffalo

Laurie Drake was in a very foul mood. She wasn't sure why; if she stopped to think about it, she'd probably have to admit that her bad stomach had something to do with it, and her lingering headache, and her two weeks now without much sleep. And the dreams. The lousy, crazy, stupid dreams. The dreams that—as lousy and crazy and stupid as they were—made her feel so very good. (And if only that good feeling could last!)

Her mother, Margaret Drake—a thin, fussy, nervous woman in her early thirties whose days were composed of cleaning, cooking, eating, watching "her stories," cooking, more cleaning, complaining, and still more cleaning, wagged a finger at Laurie. "And I don't *ever* want to hear you use that word again, young lady! Is that *very* clear?"

Sighing, Laurie said, "Yes, Mother."

"And don't you *sigh* at me, either. You're not old enough to sigh—is *that* understood?"

Laurie, after a heroic and successful effort to keep herself from sighing again, said, "Yes, I understand, Mother."

"Good." Margaret Drake put her wagging finger away. "Now you have to tell me where it was that you heard that awful word."

Laurie looked at her mother in amazement. She wanted to say, *How would that make any difference? Are you going to go and give the word back so I won't have it anymore and I won't be able to say it again?* But she knew her mother wouldn't understand that, so she said, "My stomach hurts."

Margaret Drake looked disconcerted. Then, apparently deciding that her daughter was simply evading the issue—as she often did—said, "That is *not* what we're talking about, Laurie. We are talking about the fact that you have heard the '*F*' word somewhere, and that you have used it in this house. If your father were alive, he'd thrash the living daylights out of you."

Laurie sighed again, caught herself in the middle of it, put her hand to her mouth, burped.

Margaret Drake was mortified.

Laurie burped again, louder.

Margaret Drake grew red with anger and embarrassment.

Laurie burped again, even louder, and longer, as if she'd had a half-dozen bottles of beer.

Margaret Drake slapped her. "That is not," she screeched, "a proper thing"—another slap—"for a young lady"—another slap—"to do!"

Laurie opened her mouth to burp again. But a belch—long and rolling and resonant—came out instead. And it stank, too, which astonished Margaret. It smelled like the little tins of potted meat she used to buy, until she learned what went into them. And simply as a reflex, because she had never known of any other way to control her precocious daughter, she slapped her again, then again, and again. Until, at last, Laurie reached up and caught her wrist. For the second time that morning, Margaret Drake was astonished, so astonished, in fact, that for several seconds she let Laurie hold her there, with her open hand quivering an inch or so from Laurie's face. At least she told herself that that was what she was doing—letting her daughter hold her wrist. It wasn't because Laurie had an incredibly strong grip on it. Not at all.

Margaret Drake whispered tremblingly, "You let go of me now!"

And Laurie Drake hissed back, "If you lay

a hand on me again, bitch, I'll tear your eyes out!" Then she let go of her.

Margaret stared wide-eyed at her daughter for a few seconds, then quickly left the room.

Stephen Brownleigh looked away from the viewing window in the basement of the Buffalo County Medical Examiner's Office and nodded grimly. "Yes," he said to the detective standing with him, "that's my mother. That's Vera Brownleigh."

Sergeant Guy Mallory, recently promoted, neat, pleasant-looking, put his hand comfortingly on Stephen Brownleigh's arm. "I'm very sorry," he said.

"Yes," Stephen sighed, "thank you—"

"But I must ask you to identify the other body," Sergeant Mallory interrupted.

Stephen sighed yet again, nodded, and turned back to the viewing window. On the other side of the window, a grim-faced, white-coated female lab technician lifted the sheet from the face of the second corpse. Stephen gasped and turned quickly away. There was a row of black plastic chairs nearby; he sat in one, put his face in his hands. Sergeant Mallory again laid his hand comfortingly on Stephen's arm. "Mr. Brownleigh, are you all right?"

Stephen said nothing.

The sergeant coaxed gently, "Mr. Brownleigh, are you all right? Can I get you something?"

Stephen's head, face still buried in his hands, nodded a trifle.

Mallory asked, "Is that your father, sir?"

Stephen answered into his hands, "I think so."

Mallory sat down beside him. "You think so?" His voice still was gentle. "Could it be someone else, sir?"

Stephen looked quickly at him, in astonishment. "Good Lord, Sergeant, it could be anyone, couldn't it? It could be . . . it could be *anyone*! How am I supposed to identify him? How can I identify what looks like a slab of meat, for Christ's sake!"

"Sir, it's actually just a formality—"

"A formality? My father is just a *formality*? What the hell are you—" He stopped, took a deep breath, turned his head again, planted his elbows on his thighs, clasped his hands in front of his knees. "Yes, then," he whispered, voice quaking. "Yes! It's my father—that *thing* in there is my father!"

"Thank you, sir." Mallory patted Stephen's arm. "Thank you. And you have our very sincere condolences."

"Dear Ann Landers," wrote Margaret Drake, "this is the first time I've written to you, although I've been reading your column"— She stopped, crossed out the word "column," and wrote instead "wonderful column for years." She thought a moment, the pen point stuck into her mouth, her tongue working idly at it. She went on. "But I have a problem that only a person of your credentials can help me with." She stopped, thought again, rewrote the sentence as, "But I have a problem with which only a person of your marvelous credentials can help." She liked that. She smiled, continued writing. "The problem is my daughter, whom we shall call Loretta, whom is eight"—she crossed out "eight," wrote "ten" instead—"and who is using very bad language and is also resorting to physical types of acts." She reread the letter and decided that it was going well. She wrote on. "I think you will agree with me, Ann, if I may be so bold as to call you Ann, that twelve-year-old girls"— She stopped, hurriedly crossed out the phrase "twelve-year-old girls," wrote "ten-year-old girls," and continued, "have no right whatsoever to use foul language with their mothers or to resort to physical acts against them. It is not as if they are boys, which is bad enough..." She reread the letter and decided that it sounded pretty good so far. Maybe it could stand some polishing here and there, some tightening, but it was going nicely.

She was in her bedroom, at her pink vanity table. Laurie's bedroom was right next to hers, and since the walls of the late-60s-style ranch house—in the late-60s-style subdevelopment near Orchard Park, five miles west of Buffalo—were wafer-thin, she could easily hear through them. She could hear now a string of vicious obscenities from Laurie's bedroom. She paid little attention to it; Laurie had been cursing all morning. She thought only that some of the words she was hearing had to be foreign words because she'd never heard them before.

She continued writing. "The tried and true method of stopping girls from using obscenities is to wash their little mouths out with soap, and this I have done to Laurie." She hurriedly crossed out "Laurie," wrote "Loreen," thought a moment, crossed that out, wrote "Loretta," and continued writing: "But she is still swearing 'like a trooper' as the saying goes. And there is another thing too which I think is the start of it all, and that is that she has gotten an interest in things that are supernatural, in vampires especially. I don't know why. With all this horror stuff in the movies and on TV, etcetera, I suppose it was bound to happen. My own theory, however, is that it has something to do with her father who is dead and whom she misses. She is so taken with this vampire thing that I said to her No, you may not wear a vampire costume out trick or treating this year (her last time out, of course, since she is going to be thirteen next year). I told her I thought vampires were unhealthy. So she wore a skeleton costume instead and of course when she came back to the house it was in shreds, and I had made it myself too." She stopped writing. The tone of the obscenities ushering through the wall from Laurie's room had changed. It was no longer the high whine of a twelve-year-old girl; it was a velvet drizzle tinged with hate. And by itself it was a million times more communicative than what she had been hearing before. It was communicative of murder.

She dropped her pen; it rolled to the edge of the desk and then to the pale blue shag carpet. She raised her head in nervous little fits and starts, so she was looking in the vanity's oval mirror. She saw that the bedroom door was closed, but as she watched, it opened very slowly, so slowly, in fact, that it was a good quarter minute before the naked woman who had pushed it open was revealed in the doorway.

Margaret Drake's mouth fell open. At the level of a high breathless whisper, these words escaped her. "I don't have any money."

And the naked woman said in that voice which was at once murderous and velvet and drizzly, like a razor-edge sword slicing through a melon, "You idiot, I don't want any *money*!" Then her mouth opened very wide—revealing the deadly, gleaming canines within—so she could consume as much of Margaret Drake as possible in the first bite.

But then her mouth closed partway, as if she had suddenly lost her appetite. And the electrifying aura of murder that hung about her lost some of its intensity, as if the blush of passion were leaving her, and these words, in the high pleading voice of a twelve-year-old girl vaulted across the room: "Mommy? Help me, Mommy!"

Margaret Drake's thoughts turned very briefly—more briefly than the instant necessary to blow out a candle—back to the time when her husband was alive and Laurie was a cute and bouncy toddler. Margaret remembered hearing those same words then, when the Laurie she loved most was still with her: "Mommy?" she had said in her halting, lispy toddler's voice, her little hands holding the two ends of her shoelaces, "Help me, Mommy!"

Then the instant was over and the naked woman flew across the bedroom. And because the twelve-year-old that dwelt within her had her own ideas about vampires, ideas which said that there was nothing subtle or slow or strangely loving in what they did, her wide-open mouth latched savagely onto Margaret Drake's throat and she tore a huge and quivering chunk of flesh from it.

"Whatchoo smilin' at like that for?" Hap asked the woman. "Why you smilin' like that?" He couldn't see her face well, he could see only that she was smiling, and that her eyes seemed to be on something far beyond his small stinking room.

She was naked beneath him on the lumpy mattress, and the only light in the place was from a streetlamp on the edge of what was known as "The District," an area which, forty-five years earlier, had been alive with industrial activity, manufacturing thousands of tons of war materiel, from shoes to rotor blades to toothbrushes. But when the war ended, the hub of industrial activity became merely redundant—the shoes and rotor blades and toothbrushes manufactured here, in these dozens of big square cement block buildings, were no longer needed, or were manufactured more cheaply elsewhere. So, within a couple of years, the area fell into disuse. Eventually, some of the buildings were bought by entrepreneurs, who saw them as perfect places for indoor malls, or—with major renovation—for low-cost housing. But these efforts were doomed to failure for one very good reason; the air was bad. On Buffalo's southwest side, a little more than two miles away, a hundred acres worth of smelters were kept going night and day, and since the prevailing winds were to the northeast, "The District" got the brunt of the foul air.

So now the area was all but abandoned, except for the occasional transient, bag lady, hooker, or runaway. Ironically, it was not a dangerous area to walk in because it was so desolate—even the muggers knew that the chances of making a score here were slim indeed.

The woman beneath Hap whispered, "I'm happy with my children."

It was a typically cryptic remark for her,

so Hap merely shrugged and got back to the business of "giving her a poke or two."

He did not see the small silver knife she kept in the bodice of her dress, which lay now on the floor beside the bed.

And because his mind was very much on other things, he did not see her reach and take the knife into her long, graceful fingers.

And when she traced a thin, foot-long gash into his back with the knife, he thought at first that in the throes of her passion, her fingernails were digging hard into him, so he breathed at her, "Oh baby, baby!"

She plunged the inch-long blade into the small of his back.

He stiffened on her; his mouth and eyes opened wide; small stuttering sounds came from him.

She whispered, "Oh, yes, yes—you are never more alive than when death is near! Live, live!" And she plunged the knife quickly into a buttock, then into his side, below the rib cage, then into his spine, and at last he rolled off her to the floor, where he lay on his back and twitched.

She stood above him, feet on either side of him. She leaned over, put her lips near his chest. "Live!" she breathed. "Live!" She put her lips to his chest.

He was dead five minutes later.

Chapter Five

In Boston

The desk clerk at the Ritz Carlton Hotel was losing his patience. "I'm sorry, Mr. Biergarten," he said stiffly, "but as I've told you a half-dozen times already, there is no Joan Mott Evans registered here."

Ryerson was losing patience, too. Because when Joan had been about ready to leave his house on Newbury Street and he'd asked her where in Boston she was staying, the name *Ritz Carlton* had flashed into his head as bright as neon. But now, two hours later, facing off with this thin, balding, temperamental desk clerk, he was beginning to think that Joan had tricked him.

He said, "Let me describe her to you again," although he'd described her already.

"No," the desk clerk said, "as I told you, no one of that description is registered here. And if you don't let me attend to more pressing business, sir, I will be forced to call the house detective."

Ryerson shifted Creosote from one arm to the other. It was impossible for him to tell psychically if the man was lying—hard emotion, such as the man's growing impatience, was often a barrier to reception. Ryerson had to admit anyway that the man had no reason to lie—either Joan was staying at the Ritz Carlton, or she wasn't.

The desk clerk said, "Can I assume that that will be all for the evening, sir?"

Ryerson said, "Sure. Thank you," and shifted Creosote to his other arm. He wanted to press the subject further but could think of no way to do it. "I didn't mean to bother you," he added, then went over to one of three big red leather couches in the lobby and sat down sullenly with Creosote. "Yes," he whispered to the dog, "that's precisely what she did. She tricked me." At the other end of the couch, a chubby sixtyish man in an ill-fitting gray suit speared the air with a dark wooden cane and bellowed, "I'll have no more of *that*, Falstaff!"

Ryerson glanced at him, wondered if he was doing some bastardization of Shakespeare, read from him only what appeared in his mind's eye as a mass of live reddish worms—which was often all he could read from crazies—and looked away, embarrassed because the man had caught him looking.

"Fine dog," the man said heartily, manfully, as if commenting on Ryerson's ability at arm wrestling.

Ryerson glanced at him, smiled a little, said, "Thank you," and looked away again. He didn't like dealing with public crazies. Too often when he tried to untangle what he saw moving about in their heads he became frustrated and depressed; it was like working a huge jigsaw puzzle which, when finished, formed only one piece of an almost infinitely larger puzzle. And he usually read a profound and soul-shattering despair beneath the bubbly exterior, as if a personality, a human being, had been buried alive and was slowly suffocating.

It was the same sort of thing he'd encountered six months earlier, in Rochester, New York, when his investigation into what had come to be known as "The Park Werewolf" was nearly at an end. He had the name of the murderer, but no real proof. His only proof was a desperate whisper of despair from within the innermost recesses of the murderer's brain—as if someone were calling for help from the bottom of a very deep well. It was the same sort of whisper of despair that he read now from the man at the other end of the couch. The only difference was what had overlaid it—not a mass of live reddish worms, but something stiff and black and opaque, like an iced-over river choked with pollution.

The man on the couch speared the air

again. "I'll have no more of *that*, Falstaff!" he bellowed, and within seconds a big, middle-aged, dark-haired man in a tight-fitting black suit appeared beside him, leaned over, and crooned, "Okay, Al, I think it's time for bed." He put one hand on Al's back, the other on his wrist, and helped him to his feet.

Ryerson said, "Pardon me, but is he registered here?"

The big man looked critically at Ryerson. "Who's asking?"

Ryerson shook his head as an apology for butting in. "No one. I'm just curious."

"He's my friend," the man said, and turned his attention back to Al. "C'mon, Al. Big day tomorrow."

Ryerson began, "It's just that—"

"Who's he hurtin'?" the big man cut in. "He ain't hurtin' no one. All he does is sit here and talk to himself. So what? I seen you talking to yourself a few minutes ago."

And Ryerson, regretting his words immediately, said, "Yes, I know, but for his own good—"

The beefy man said, "What's for his own good is between him and me, 'cuz we're friends, you know. I look after him, and he looks after me, when he can. Just because he's sick don't mean he ain't my friend no more, and it don't mean I don't know how he feels inside. Shit, you put him away and he'd die in a month. At least here he's got me; we got each other."

Ryerson wanted to say, *That's a hell of a speech*, but he knew the man would mistake it for sarcasm, so he said, "Yes, I agree, I'm sorry," and watched as the two of them made their way slowly—Al as if in pain—to the elevators.

In Buffalo

"Now *why'd* I do that?!" mumbled Sergeant Guy Mallory.

His partner, Gail Newman, looked over at him from her desk, grinned, and said, "Do what?"

He grimaced. "This *stupid* thing." He held up a white paper cup, put it back on his desk, grimaced again. "My wife's after me to take vitamins, you know. Vitamin A especially, because I've got this skin problem and vitamin A is supposed to be good for that, she says."

"The eyes, too," Gail said. "Carrots have a lot of vitamin A. So do fish."

Mallory harrumphed. "Tell me about it. I got these fish oil capsules and I thought, *Why don't I put them in the coffee*—"

"Why would you do that?"

"Well, you know," he explained haltingly, as if embarrassed, "some people don't like to take pills. Hell, Gail, they glom up right here." He pointed at a spot just above his Adam's apple. "So I thought, why not put them in the coffee?"

Gail chuckled. "And now the coffee tastes like fish, right?"

"Damn right!" he said, and dumped the cup of fishy-tasting coffee into the wastebasket.

Gail laughed. "You're a scream sometimes, Mallory. Did you know that?"

"Yeah," he said glumly. "I know it." He sighed, nodded at a file folder on her desk. "Did you get anything from the neighbors, Gail?" That afternoon—it was close to 5:00 now—she had gone to interview John and Vera Brownleigh's next-door neighbors while Mallory kept a 3:00 P.M. court date. She'd gotten back from the interviews less than five minutes earlier. She shook her head. "Nothing substantial. One of the neighbors"—she checked her notepad—"a Mrs. Garfungle—"

"Garfungle? With a 'g'? Are you sure?"

Gail nodded. "Yes. I thought it was Garfunkel, too, but she corrected me. Anyway, she says that she heard loud talking at"—she checked her notebook—"at 10:45 on the night of the murders."

"Uh-huh," Mallory said. "How close is she to the Brownleigh house?"

"Mrs. Garfungle? Fifty feet or so."

"And did she have her windows open?"

Gail hesitated, then answered, "I don't know. I didn't ask. Is it important?"

Mallory shrugged. "Not really. It's just that if she didn't have her windows open, and the Brownleighs didn't have theirs open either—and it *was* the end of October—then the 'loud talking' she heard had to have been very loud." He hesitated. "Louder, I mean, than a simple argument. Do you follow me?"

Gail nodded. "Yes, Mallory. I follow you."

She looked a little miffed, Mallory thought; he said, "I didn't mean to interrupt. Go ahead."

She flipped a page of her notebook. "I asked her if she could make out any single words or sentences. She said no. Only loud talking. She said it was nothing new, that they argued quite a lot apparently—"

"And what do you think of that, Gail?"

"Think of what?"

"Of the fact that this Garfungle woman said that the Brownleighs argued a lot."

"I don't know," Gail answered. "I guess I'd have to wonder why she'd notice the time of this particular argument."

"And?"

"And I'd have to wonder if there was something different about it that would *make* her notice the time." Mallory saw a small grin appear and disappear quickly on Gail's lips. She went on. "And wondering that, I guess I'd have to ask her to think about it. I'd have to say to her, 'Just try and remember what you heard, Mrs. Garfungle. Was it pretty much the same as their other arguments, or was there something different about it?'" She hesitated; Mallory sighed. She went on. "And, of course, that's what I asked her."

Mallory sighed again. "Okay, okay, so I'm a bastard—what else is new? Just tell me what this Mrs. Garfinkle, Garfunkle, whatever—Gar*fungle* said, okay?"

Gail smiled coyly at him. "You're not a bastard, Mallory. You're just taking your promotion a little too seriously." She hesitated, went on. "Mrs. Garfungle said, and I quote, 'Yes. There was something different about it, young lady. There were three voices. Not two. Three. Two women, and him, Mr. Brownleigh.'"

Mallory's phone rang. He snatched it up. "Mallory here," he said. After a few moments he said, "Yes, thanks, we'll be there in twenty minutes," and hung up. He said to Gail, "We've got another one."

"Another one?"

"Another one like the Brownleighs."

"Shit," Gail said. "Who?"

"Some woman named Drake; she lives up near Orchard Park." He hesitated, then pushed himself heavily, wearily, to his feet. "Dammit, Gail—her daughter found her, for Christ's sake—her twelve-year-old daughter found her!"

In the Records Division of the Buffalo Police Department, Irene Sabitch again sat scowling at her computer monitor, and, again, her coworker Glen Coffman looked over and told her she looked like she'd just chomped down on a clove of garlic.

"It's this same damned file directory," she said, eyes glued to the screen. "I put the whole thing aside, you know, the other day. I didn't want to mess with it. But I went and got that list of user numbers you mentioned, and I inputted all of them—"

"*All* of them?" Glen asked, astonished. "How many were there?"

"Seventeen hundred and eighty-six," she answered. "Of course, the computer helped me."

"Oh. Yes, of course."

"But none of them work."

"None of them?"

"None of them. So I called upstairs to Homicide—"

"How do you know it's a Homicide file?"

"I don't." She glanced at him. "But I had to start somewhere, didn't I?"

He nodded. "Sure."

She looked back at her monitor. "And they don't have any hard copies on anyone named 'Curtis, L.' or 'Hawkins' "—she was referring to two of the file names—"so I called Vice, and I called a couple of other precincts, and no one seems to have a hard copy on any of this stuff."

Glen shook his head knowingly. "That can't be, Irene. And I'll tell you why—"

"I know why."

"I'll tell you anyway. It can't be because *everyone* has a personal user number—whether they use it or not—and every case on the subsystem has a duplicate hard file *somewhere*. The subsystem files, Irene—"

"I know," she interrupted, "the subsystem files come from the hard copies."

"That's right."

"Then I'd assume, Glen, that someone has been messing with the hard copies."

"Sure," he said, "I'd assume that, too."

"So now," she said, "all I've got to find out is who, and then we can nail his ass to the wall!"

Chapter Six

In Boston

Ryerson Biergarten did many things on impulse. He'd married Coreen on impulse, and it had turned out to be a mistake. He'd bought his first house on impulse—after *Conversations with Charlene* topped the country's best seller lists—and got taken. It was an old farmhouse just outside Boston which the owner swore was in top condition. And Ryerson, trusting his hunches, and reading nothing but goodwill from the man, bought it. It was six months later that he discovered the dry rot, and the leaky roof, when its temporary patches gave way, and the equally leaky cellar walls, whose equally temporary patches had also given way. It was then that Ryerson resolved to remember that some people could lie with goodwill not only on their lips but in their hearts as well.

Most of his impulses, however, proved out.

His '48 Ford wagon—known as a "Woody" because of the genuine wood paneling along the doors and rear quarter panels—was one of those impulses. He hadn't bought the car merely because it was an antique. He couldn't have cared less about its age *per se*. He'd bought it because it was full of happy memories that he could feel and taste and enjoy as strongly as anyone else experienced the *smell* of a new car. He found that those memories faded over time, as if, he theorized, he'd somehow coaxed them away with the memories that were piling up in his own life. But, happily, they did not fade altogether. What remained after two years was like the faint odor of a delicate perfume that lingers in a room long after the woman wearing it has gone. It made driving the car a distinct pleasure. It was, he admitted—moving along the Massachusetts Turnpike at fifty miles per hour, the car's top speed—the only thing that made driving it a pleasure. Not only was it slow, it also handled like a truck, which it was, in essence, and its suspension system was long past due for an overhaul. (He'd been waiting six months now for the right parts. "Car that old," the mechanic told him, "ain't a jiffy to get parts for, you know.") He was on his way to Buffalo. His hunch was that Joan Mott Evans was already back there, and if she wasn't, he'd surprise her.

The main thing pushing him to Buffalo

was what he had sensed in Joan during her visit to his house on Newbury Street. He had sensed *love* in her, very clearly—the love she had for her dead friend, Lila, and the love she had simply for being alive. She was, Ryerson thought, a woman whose very existence had love as its focus. It was that love, he thought, that had made her do to Lila what she had, ultimately, decided she had to do.

He'd also sensed that Joan saw a connection between Lila Curtis and what had happened in Rochester. For months now he'd suspected that there was a connection, though he wasn't certain what it was, exactly. With Joan's help, perhaps he could find out.

Most of all, he wanted to know if what had happened in Rochester was simply some strange and singular twist of reality. Or if it was repeatable. If, perhaps, it was being repeated even as he drove south down the Massachusetts Turnpike.

He reached over and gave Creosote, asleep on the passenger's seat, a few long, slow, loving strokes. The dog grumbled in its sleep, wheezed, snorted, fell silent. Ryerson put his hand back on the wheel—the wagon was too hard to control with just one hand. He was happy to be leaving the city for a few days. He loved Boston; it was his home, it would always be his home. But it was still a city. And the continual barrage of psychic input in any city was almost deafening at times. It wasn't bad if he stayed in the house, or went walking very early, when most of the city's people were asleep, or in the mid-evening, when most of its people had been sated by a good meal and were camped in front of the tube with their minds on hold. But if he had to go out on a weekday, when the streets were teeming with people, what escaped their minds and shot into his—all their worries and joys and complaints—had more than once driven him back to his house. He thought he knew how an agoraphobic felt at such times. There was a way to shut out most of the input; he simply erected a mental wall made of bricks and mortar—much as the adults in the movie *Village of the Damned* had done to ward off the psychic probing of their unearthly children. But he didn't like to do that because then he had to rely solely on his five senses to gauge the world around him. He wasn't used to using only five senses; he'd used six senses since birth. So, when he erected that mental brick wall, he felt cut off from all that was going on around him, the same way a sighted man feels when the room he's in is suddenly darkened.

Now, at a little past 7:00 on the Massachusetts Turnpike, thirty miles south of Boston, he got an occasional short psychic blast as cars zipped by—sometimes what he got was coherent, a sentence or two, and sometimes it was merely a brief feeling of pleasure, or a smell, or pain. Quite often he got nothing at all, and he would think momentarily, at such times, that he'd suddenly lost his psychic ability. It was his greatest fear—that he would wake up one morning to discover that the gift he'd been given at birth had been taken from him. If that did happen, he'd decided, then he'd have to look upon the loss as eminently fair; after all, he'd still have the use of five senses, and that was as much as anyone was entitled to. Still, he had to admit that he'd sooner lose his hearing or his sight than his ability to know, if usually just at random, what was going on in the minds of those around him.

He stroked Creosote again, felt the wagon drift right, toward the guard rail, steered left with both hands. He whispered, "What's the matter, Woody? Tie rods going?" And he thought, not for the first time, how nice it would be if he could peer into the hearts of machines, too. And that brought up what, for him, was the old saw that he could not peer into *hearts* so much as into *heads*. He was, he imagined, much like the fledgling computer programmer who had gotten to the point where he could write and read very complex programs but had little idea how the lines and commands and algorithms he wrote were interpreted and acted upon by the machine itself. His experience buying his first house had proved that; and so had his experience dealing with the poor demented creature responsible for the murders in Rochester. That damned soul had proved dramatically that some people—many people, perhaps—were able to use the output of their brains to hide what was going on in their hearts, even from people like Ryerson. Even, amazingly, from themselves.

Ryerson wondered if Joan Mott Evans was such a person. He didn't think so. He supposed that if he were still a betting man, he'd have put very high odds against it. But the simple fact that he had asked the question proved that there was indeed a question, a doubt. And that doubt was yet another reason he was going back to Buffalo.

In Buffalo

Gail Newman liked her work. Most of it, anyway. The challenge in homicide investigation was often—though by no means always—to outwit the murderer, and she'd been able to do that with an amazing degree of success. She was, in fact, the youngest female candidate for promotion to sergeant in the history of the Buffalo Police Department; it was a promotion which had, for various internal reasons, gone to her partner, Guy Mallory, instead.

She did not, however, like the physical act of examining victims. She wasn't squeamish—at least no more so than any of her colleagues, and far less than some. She had, instead, a highly developed sense of what was private. A person's body and a person's anguish were very private. So the victim of a murder—who had had his or her privacy violated in a terribly overt and ultimate way—should not have to suffer the indignity of still more violation. Never mind that a murder victim was, rationally, beyond suffering and anguish and violation. Rationally, the victim was merely a slab of flesh and hair and bone that the medical examiner could saw into and probe about in while making quick, grisly jokes to no one in particular. Rationally, the victim had ceased being a person at all. But that was, of course—as Gail bent over the body of Margaret Drake—just the sort of rational thinking that was all but impossible at times like these. There, for instance, were the victim's hands—long and graceful-looking, the ends of the red-polished nails chipped slightly. Maybe they were hands that had once drifted lovingly and beautifully over the keys of a piano. Or maybe they'd tried and had been found wanting. But they wouldn't try anymore. And there were the victim's eyes. Open halfway. With a soft glaze on them. What had they seen that morning, for instance, when they'd fluttered open from sleep? The usual and familiar things, no doubt. A nightstand. A clock radio. A window, curtains open; sunlight. A new day—better than yesterday, perhaps. Not as good as tomorrow.

Gail heard from above her, "She's a real mess, isn't she?" It was Mallory's voice.

Gail had yet to focus fully on the great gaping hole at the side of the woman's neck. "Yes," she whispered, and turned her head to look up at Mallory. "A real mess." A police photographer appeared, asked, "Can I get in here now?" Gail said, glancing stiffly at him, "No. Not yet. A few minutes, okay?"

The photographer shrugged, said, "Okay," then said something about the body "not going anywhere anyway," which was his standard line, and backed off.

Gail looked again at Margaret Drake's body. She focused on the gaping hole at the side of the woman's neck. There was, strangely, very little blood around the body, or even around that awful wound, possibly, Gail thought, because a wound like that would have caused the woman to go into shock, and thus inhibit the flow of blood. The M.E. would have a better answer, no doubt. She said, eyes still on the wound, "It's not as bad as the male victim's, though. It's not as bad as Mr. Brownleigh was."

"It's bad enough," Mallory said.

Gail turned from the body, started for the

door, looked back at Mallory. "I'm going to talk to the daughter. You coming?"

Mallory shook his head. "No. The two of us will scare her, I think. You go ahead. I think she'd probably rather talk to a woman anyway."

Andrew Spurling, Detective Third Grade

Andrew Spurling, thirty-two, was tall, well-built, average-looking, which is to say that his face could have been an amalgamation of male faces at a football game or wrestling match. He had no hobbies, although he was very attentive of his gun, a Smith and Wesson .38.

His record at the Buffalo Police Department was unremarkable. He'd been a little over a year with the force, and in that time had not distinguished himself in any way, good or bad. He was a run-of-the-mill cop who did his job and tried to stay out of the way. That had not always been his attitude; as a child in Syracuse, New York, he was known as the toughest kid on the block. That toughness did not transfer in any meaningful way to his work at the Buffalo Police Department. He was usually assigned the job of picking up people who'd written bad checks in amounts of under $100. Such checks constituted a class A misdemeanor, not a felony, which usually put the bad-check artist in the easy-to-handle category. Detective Spurling was not astoundingly happy with this kind of work, but he was willing to do it because it was work, after all.

Occasionally, he fantasized about being twelve years old, growing up in Syracuse, New York, when he was top dog and people did what *he* told them to do.

Chapter Seven

Laurie Drake was sitting on the edge of her bed with her arms and ankles crossed and her head lowered. She was wearing blue jeans, and a white pleated blouse with puffed short sleeves which, Gail thought, made her look appreciably older than her twelve years.

Gail stopped just inside the doorway. "Hello," she said gently. Laurie looked up at once, as if surprised, sighed heavily, lowered her head again. She said nothing. Gail went over, stood for a few moments next to her, then sat beside her on the bed. "Your name's Laurie, isn't it?"

"Yes," Laurie whispered.

"My name's Gail Newman, Laurie. I'm with the Buffalo Police Department. Do you think you're up to answering a few questions?"

Laurie looked confusedly at Gail. Gail went on. "If you'd rather wait, that's okay." She paused. "*Would* you rather wait?"

Laurie shook her head a little. "No," she whispered. She asked, "Is my mother dead?"

Gail wasn't much taken aback by the question. In one form or another, of course, it was a pretty common question among a victim's close relatives. "Yes," she answered. "Your mother's dead. I'm very sorry."

Laurie continued looking confusedly at her for a few seconds. Then she nodded as if in acceptance and said, "Yes, I thought so." A pause. "I mean, she *looked* dead." She lowered her head again. Gail heard her begin to sniffle, as if on the verge of tears. She patted Laurie's elbow. "I'm sorry, this isn't a good time." She stood. "We'll talk later—"

Laurie looked quickly up at her. "Someone ate her, didn't they, Miss Newman?"

Gail wasn't certain she saw a grin flit across Laurie's mouth. If she had seen a grin, she thought, it, too, would not be the first time. She shook her head vehemently. "No. No one . . . did that to your mother!"

Laurie said, "She said that that was okay. She said that's how you got life back."

"I don't understand, Laurie. Who said that?"

Laurie cocked her pretty head. "And that's what it looked like, Miss Newman. It looked like someone ate her." She pointed at the exposed part of her neck. "Right here. Didn't you see that?"

Gail said nothing for a moment. She thought this was going to be awfully tough. "Yes, I saw that," she said, and sat on the bed again. Laurie turned her head to look at Gail intensely as Gail went on. "And I think what we're dealing with here, Laurie, is some kind of dog. A large dog."

Laurie nodded. "You mean like a guard dog or something?"

"Yes. Like a guard dog."

Laurie shook her head. "But we don't have one of those, Miss Newman. All we have is a cat. It's not even a big cat."

"Yes, I know." Gail had seen the cat resting on a kitchen counter; it was a small white longhaired cat with a red collar. "What we're talking about is someone else's—"

"My dad hated her."

Gail was confused. "Your dad hated your mother?"

Laurie grinned broadly, as if very amused. "No. Not my mother. The cat. He tried to kill it once. He threw it out the second floor window."

"Oh," Gail said noncommittally. Then, "Where is your father?"

Laurie's grin vanished. "He's dead," she said matter-of-factly. "Just like my mom."

Gail found herself getting nervous. She wasn't sure why. Odd reactions among a victim's relatives were commonplace, and Laurie's reactions were actually no odder than others she'd encountered. She remembered, especially, the elderly man whose wife stuck her head into an oven and asphyxiated herself a year earlier. When she and Mallory got to the man's house, in answer to a call from the man's grandson, they found that the man had put foiled-wrapped potatoes around the woman's head, and a nice meat loaf on the shelf just beneath. "Well," the man explained heartily, "as soon as my wife gets her head out of the oven we can all eat." That had been pretty damned odd, she thought. So, if this young girl seemed to be seesawing back and forth between tears and *so-what* about her mother's murder, then it was only because the human mind is a very complex and fragile thing.

Gail said, "When did you find your mother, Laurie?"

"When I got home from school," Laurie answered, still matter-of-factly.

"And that was when?"

"About three-thirty."

Gail got her notebook from her purse, wrote "3:30" in it. She asked, "And did you notice anything odd then? When you came home."

"You mean in the house?"

"Not particularly."

"What you mean is, did I notice any strange cars on the street."

Gail nodded. "Yes. Or people."

"Or dogs?" She grinned again.

Gail hesitated, then said, "Did you?"

"No."

"Nothing at all? Try to think back, Laurie; see yourself coming home again, down the street. What's the first thing you see when you get off the bus?"

"Timmy Wheelock."

"Timmy Wheelock? Is he your . . . boyfriend?"

"No, but he wants to be. He waits for me on the corner every day after school. And he follows me home." She looked suddenly excited. "Do you think he's dangerous, Miss Newman? Do you think he's going to try and hurt me?"

Gail chose not to answer that question. She said instead, "Does he follow you all the way home, Laurie?"

"No," she answered, sounding suddenly weary of the conversation.

"How far does he follow you?"

"Halfway. He's got a paper route."

"Oh, and he's got to get home to take care of it?"

"No. He's got to finish it."

"You mean, he doesn't ride the bus with you?"

"No. His father picks him up at three. That's when school gets out."

Gail nodded. "Do you know Timmy's address, Laurie?" Her idea was that Timmy, if he did indeed follow Laurie every day from the bus stop, could think of something that Laurie hadn't.

Laurie shrugged. "For all I know, he lives in a hole in the ground. The big creep, the asshole!"

Gail said, embarrassed, "I see," and decided to get off the subject of Timmy; how many Wheelocks could there be in Orchard Park, after all? He'd be easy enough to find if it became necessary. "After Timmy went home—" she began, and Laurie interrupted.

"He rides a moped."

"Yes. Good. Thank you. So after he drove off on his moped, and you were alone—"

"He looks like a fucking *jerk* on it. Christ, he's sixteen years old and six feet tall and his knees stick up and he looks like a fucking jerk!"

"Yes," Gail said, "but I think we're getting off the subject—"

"Do you have a boyfriend, Miss Newman?"

Gail sighed.

Mallory appeared in the doorway and cleared his throat; Gail looked up at him. "Yes?" she said, her annoyance obvious.

"Can I talk to you, Gail? Out here?"

Gail looked quickly at Laurie, then back at Mallory. "Right now? Can't it wait?"

"No. It can't." He sounded very firm.

"Okay," Gail said; then to Laurie, "I'll be back in a few moments, Laurie. You going to be all right?"

Laurie nodded brightly. "Sure. Why not?"

To which Gail could say only, "Yes. Good," then she left the room to speak with Mallory in the hallway.

He said, his voice low, "The kid's lying, Gail."

"Oh?"

"Yes. I just talked to the M.E. The woman's been dead for at least twenty-four hours."

Gail took a deep breath. "Jesus Christ," she breathed, "I hate this."

"Join the club, sweet cheeks."

"Please don't call me that, Guy." A pause. "Okay, who's going to do it?"

Mallory, putting on his magnanimous look, offered, "Well, since I'm the senior officer here—"

"The hell with that," Gail cut in. "You'll scare the crap out of her. I'll do it." And she went back into Laurie's bedroom and told her, "Laurie, I'm afraid you're going to have to come with me."

"Am I under arrest?" She seemed strangely unconcerned, even a little pleased.

Gail shook her head. "No. You're not under arrest, Laurie. But I do have to remind you of your constitutional rights." She was not, she realized, doing this by the book.

Laurie said, "You mean like I have the right to remain silent, and the right to have an attorney present and all that stuff?"

Gail extended her hand. "Yes, Laurie." Laurie took her hand, stood. Gail told her her rights. "Do you understand?"

"Sure." Laurie glanced quickly around her room. It was a very girlish room, thanks to her mother. The colors were all soft pastels, the bedclothes frilly, the furniture properly dainty-looking. She said, "This is really awful, isn't it, Miss Newman?"

Gail answered after a few moments. "Perhaps you should bring a change of clothes, Laurie. Why don't I give you a moment to do that, okay?"

Laurie answered, "Who's going to take care of Magic?"

"The cat? That's his name—Magic?"

"Uh-huh. He can't feed himself, you know."

Gail put her hand comfortingly on Laurie's arm. "I'll take care of him, Laurie. He can keep my cat company."

"He's mean, you know. He's real mean. I'll bet you he's the one that killed my mother."

Gail let her hand drop. She nodded at the doorway. "I'll be out there waiting for you, Laurie." She glanced quickly around the room. Two windows; she'd have to tell a uniform to watch them. "I'll close the door to give you some privacy. You've got five minutes." And she turned and left the room.

Five minutes later she knocked on the door. "Laurie," she called, "I'm sorry, but it's time to go." She waited, got no answer, knocked briefly again. She pushed the door open.

The room was empty.

Benny Bloom

At Buffalo Pierpont High School Benjamin Bloom (who much preferred the name "Benny") was almost universally thought of as "a nerd," especially by other nerds, who regarded the term as a badge of honor.

Benny couldn't help being a nerd. He was very smart, loved poetry—especially the poetry of T. S. Eliot—and had a natural shyness that made him look clumsy and ineffectual. His hobbies included stamp collecting, butterfly collecting (he waited for the butterflies to die a natural death because he couldn't bear the thought of killing them), astrophysics, and, of course, poetry. At sixteen and a half his attraction to the opposite sex was in full bloom, so to speak, although he was yet to, as he told his closest male friends, "relieve myself of my cumbersome virginity."

Part Two

Chapter Eight

Two Days Later

Ryerson was rifling through the Yellow Pages of the Buffalo telephone book in search of veterinarians open twenty-four hours a day. It was 1:30 in the morning. At a little past 12:00, Creosote had begun to whimper pitifully. A half hour later he crawled over to a corner of the motel room, plopped down, still whimpering, and began to breathe very shallowly, and quickly. Ryerson was sure that each of those short, shallow breaths was going to be his last.

Ryerson slammed the telephone book closed with a thud. "Nuts!" he whispered. There were no veterinarians open twenty-four hours a day, at least none that advertised in the Yellow Pages.

He went over to Creosote, got down on his haunches, gently stroked him. "It's okay, fella," he whispered. "You're going to be all right; I won't let anything happen to you." Creosote's quick breathing slowed, though only for a moment, as if his master's soothing words had temporarily eased his anxiety.

Ryerson shook his head. "Dammit, dog; why can't I *read* you?" It wasn't entirely true that he couldn't read Creosote. He usually got something like the snow between channels on a TV set. But from time to time, though very fleetingly, he got a feeling of unbridled and unreasoning joy—the response of an animal to health, and life, and the unquestioned fact of its immortality.

Now he was getting only snow, and something that felt vaguely like pain or pressure that was impossible to grab hold of—each time he tried, it slipped away. He straightened. He knew that his only recourse was to put Creosote in the Woody and drive around until he found a vet whose office was in his home and wake him up.

He gently lifted Creosote into his arms. "It's okay, fella," he crooned. "It's okay; we'll get you fixed up."

Joan Mott Evans decided that she wasn't hungry after all; she closed her refrigerator door. There wasn't much to eat anyway. Some plain yogurt—which, at 2:00 in the morning, wasn't terribly appealing—a few stalks of celery, a jar of Hain's 100% Pure and Natural Peanut Butter, and half a loaf of Hollywood Dark Bread that should have been given to the birds a week ago.

She sat at the small round kitchen table and poked idly with her fingernail at a hardened drop of spaghetti sauce that had escaped her desultory efforts at cleaning.

She thought, *What did Jimmy Carter call it?—A "malaise of the spirit"?* She whispered, "Well, I've got it, Jimmy." Damn, but if her trip to Boston hadn't gone so badly! Damn, but if Ryerson Biergarten hadn't turned out to be such a crud! Damn, but if she didn't have to hide this . . . *thing* inside her head for the rest of her life; if only she could share it. That would make it easier to bear, of course. Sharing guilt always made it easier to bear. She didn't know why, but it did.

The kitchen was dark. She preferred it that way. She wasn't up to appliance pastels and knotty pine cupboards and the Corning Range Top at the moment.

She wondered what she would be doing if one of her succession of boyfriends—or, better yet, a compilation of them all—were here with her at that moment. Would he be trying to coax the reason for her "malaise of the spirit" from her? Probably. He'd probably be trying to make a joke of it—"Mayonnaise of the spirit," he'd say. "Goes great with sliced turkey." And she'd say, trying mightily to smile, "Okay, turkey, where would you like to be sliced?" which he'd try hard to interpret as merely a good-natured joke, although he'd insist on seeing something cutting and personal in it (and, of course, there would be something cutting and personal in it). After a while he'd lean back in the small wooden chair, with his hands behind his head, and he'd observe sagely, "Let's get some light on this," and stand and turn on the overhead light. "Shed light on a problem," he'd say as he sat back down, "and you go a long way toward solving it."

She smiled as these thoughts came to her; as far as she was concerned, all of her boyfriends had been losers. She pursed her lips. No, they weren't losers—they had turned out, merely, to be right for someone else, not her.

She dismissed her succession of boyfriends with a self-critical smile and a shake of the head.

Like Ryerson Biergarten, she enjoyed the very early morning—it was just past 2:00—when the psychic atmosphere had only a light breeze in it, a breeze stirred up, mostly, by night creatures on the prowl—tomcats, owls, the occasional raccoon or opossum, both of which had, in the past decade or so, grown bold enough to make regular forays this far into the outskirts of the city. Most of the occasional psychic drifts she got from these creatures were pleasant because they were so simple and guileless, and—like Creosote—often an open and tingling expression of joy at the mere fact of being alive. At other times, and for blessedly brief moments, she got a whiff of naked and screeching terror; she'd see the ground moving rapidly away from her, she'd feel a heavy wind on her back, then an instant of tremendous, scorching pain. She knew what caused this. In the thirty acres of open fields behind her house there were probably ten thousand field mice and a hundred cottontail rabbits. And in the maple trees ringing the fields there were probably a half-dozen owls who nightly swooped silently down, grabbed one of the hapless mice or one of the baby cottontails in its talons, and just as silently carried it off to be swallowed whole at the nest.

It was only when a car passed by on the road fifty feet in front of the house or when one of her neighbors got up because of insomnia that her good feeling, her sense of peace and aloneness, was dulled. Because the input she sometimes received then—though most of the time, because her powers were in their infancy, she received nothing at all— was the same sort of complex worrying, and yearning, and questioning that she got randomly when she went into the city.

Ryerson Biergarten, Creosote cradled lovingly in his arms, knocked loudly for the fifth time on the massive oak door. On the doorjamb there was a six inch by three inch brass plate which read "Craig Gibson, D.V.M." Below that there was a doorbell, and just below the doorbell there was a piece of notepaper taped to the wood with the words

"Please Knock Loud" written on it in a childish hand.

Creosote was not doing at all well. His shallow breathing had grown even shallower, and his respiration had doubled.

Ryerson knocked loudly again. Then he yelled, "C'mon, for Lord's sake! Get out of bed!" He knew—he could sense it—that the big Victorian house was occupied. Three people, he guessed. A man, two women; one of the women was young, maybe a teenager.

He saw a light go on in a second floor window. Then the window was pushed open and a male head appeared. "What the hell do you want? Do you have any idea what time it is?"

Ryerson called back, "My dog's very sick. Can you help him?"

The man, whose head was backlit so Ryerson could not see his features well, hesitated, then called, "Is it urgent?"

Ryerson thought, *No, I do this sort of thing as a hobby!* "Yes," he called, "it's very urgent. Please help him!"

The man was opening the front door a minute later.

In Buffalo, at 98 Delaware Avenue, in a three-room, second floor apartment, in a house that had four similar apartments, Gail Newman was awakened from sleep by what she thought at first was a cat fight. Since she'd brought Laurie Drake's cat, Magic, home two days earlier (it didn't matter that Laurie, still missing, was technically a fugitive—a promise was a promise after all, and, as Laurie had said, the cat couldn't feed itself) it and her own cat, Thomas, had fought at least a dozen times. Thomas was usually the instigator, since the apartment was his home turf, but Magic always made a good showing of himself, although Thomas was nearly twice his size.

Gail sat up in the twin bed, turned on the bedside lamp, and scanned the small room. "Okay, you two!" she hissed. "Can it or you're both going outside." Then she saw that Thomas was asleep in his usual spot, on a small upholstered club chair in one corner of the room. As she watched, he lifted his head and squinted sleepily at her.

Then she heard the high, squeaky, extended ring of the doorbell (which, from the vantage point of sleep, she realized, could easily sound like a cat fight).

"Damn," she whispered, swung her feet off the bed, stood unsteadily, got her yellow robe from the back of the door, and went grumbling into the living room. The doorbell sounded again just as she put her finger on the intercom button. "Yes?" she said.

"Miss Newman?"

A woman's voice, she thought, and said again, "Yes?"

"Miss Newman?" the voice repeated.

No, Gail corrected herself; the voice sounded

more like the voice of a young girl—it was hard to be sure over the intercom. "Who is this, please?" she asked.

"Are you there?"

"Who *is* this?" Gail insisted. *Yes*, she thought, *it is the voice of a young girl*. Maybe some local kid trying to be funny; within the next few moments the girl might quip, *Is your refrigerator running?*

"Can I come up?" asked the voice.

"Not until you tell me who you are and what you want," Gail answered.

A short pause, then, "I'm hurt, Miss Newman. Can you help me? I'm hurt," and Gail heard what she supposed was a twinge of pain in the girl's tone, although, again, the squawk of the intercom made it difficult to be sure of anything.

Gail said, "What happened to you?"

Silence.

"What happened to you?" Gail repeated. "How are you hurt?"

She heard a soft, quick giggle, then, "I've been raped, Miss Newman."

Gail hesitated, uncertain. Then she said, "That's nothing to joke about, young lady—"

"It's true," the girl insisted, "it's true! I've been raped, my boyfriend raped me!"

And Gail, convinced, said, "Open the door when you hear the buzzer."

Dr. Craig Gibson, D.V.M., said, looking very confused, "As close as I can tell, Mr.

Biergarten, your dog has suffered a severe asthmatic attack."

They were in the doctor's examination room, in the east wing of the big Victorian house. Creosote, breathing normally, lay asleep and heavily sedated on a stainless steel examining table between them.

Ryerson said, "Pardon me, Doctor, but I know when he's having an asthma attack—"

"Yes, I'm sure you do, Mr. Biergarten. I'm just giving you what I'll admit is professional guesswork. If you'd like to leave the dog with me for a day or so, I can do some workups on him and then give you something a bit more definitive."

Ryerson considered the proposal for a moment, then shook his head. "No," he said, "thank you. He seems to be all right now."

"The symptoms could recur at any time," Gibson warned, "so I really think that for the dog's own good—"

Ryerson shook his head, lifted Creosote from the examining table. Moments earlier he'd read something very unpleasant from Dr. Craig Gibson, D.V.M. He'd read that the man hated dogs. "No, thanks," Ryerson said, trying hard for a tone of cordial apology. "I appreciate your efforts, though." He shifted Creosote carefully to one arm, reached into the inside breast pocket of his gray tweed sport coat. "Will you take a check?"

* * *

The knock at Gail Newman's door was a soft triple knock that she answered at once.

She found Laurie Drake smiling up at her from the hallway. "Hello, Miss Newman," Laurie said. "I wasn't really raped." And her smile increased.

Gail reached quickly, caught Laurie's arm, pulled her into the apartment, locked and bolted the door. She turned sharply to Laurie. She began hotly, "You brat! You goddamned brat—"

Laurie broke into a fit of sobbing.

"Jesus Christ!" Gail breathed, led her to the couch, and sat down beside her. After a moment Gail said, "I'm sorry, Laurie. I lost my temper. I don't like jokes about rape. Please understand." Laurie continued sobbing; her head was lowered, her face was in her hands, and her shoulders heaved with each sob. Gail went on. "Do you want something, Laurie? Some water?"

Laurie continued sobbing. Beneath the sobs Gail thought she heard what sounded like cloth ripping.

Laurie's cat, Magic, trotted into the room from the kitchen, came over to Laurie and rubbed against her ankles. Gail said, "There's your cat, Laurie. Say hi."

The sound of cloth ripping was more pronounced now, Gail realized. And the tone of Laurie's sobbing had changed, too—there were short bursts of what sounded like laughter in it.

Gail put her hand on Laurie's arm. "I'm going to have to call the Department, Laurie. You understand why, don't you?"

The white pleated blouse with puffed sleeves that Laurie was wearing ripped down the sides.

Gail stood abruptly.

Laurie's head came up from her hands. Her gaze fell on Gail.

Gail gasped, "Who are you?"

And the woman on the couch breathed, "You asked what I wanted. I want *you*, Detective Newman."

Gail backed toward her bedroom door. She kept her service revolver in the bedroom, in the drawer of the little nightstand.

The woman on the couch stood. The bottom of the shredded blouse came halfway up her stomach, and the jeans were raggedly torn down the inner seams—she looked for all the world, Gail thought frantically, confusedly, like a cover illustration for some torrid and kinky romance.

"Laurie?" she managed. "You need help; let me call someone." She was at her bedroom door now.

The woman advancing on her across the small living room said, sneering, "The only thing I need right now is you, Detective." And she opened her mouth to reveal the huge white canines within.

"God in heaven," Gail whispered, and launched herself into the bedroom toward the little nightstand. She hit the side of the bed with her stomach. A gust of air and a quick "Uhh!" of pain and surprise escaped her. She doubled over, fell backward to the floor, saw the woman standing victoriously above her, scrambled up, fumbled for the drawer pull, felt an incredibly strong hand on her neck, pulled the drawer open.

Chapter Nine

Some things happen purely by coincidence. A woman whose mortgage is two months past due and whose kid's shoes are too tight because she can't afford new ones wins the New York State Lottery purely by coincidence. And, purely by coincidence, a man decides not to board a plane and learns a couple of hours later that it crashed with no survivors. Another man leaves for work two minutes later than usual, for whatever reason, and is broadsided by a runaway bus that would have been two minutes behind him had he left for work at his usual time.

All by coincidence. Chance. Which, like gravity, is a force that no one understands completely.

And so it was purely by coincidence as well that Ryerson Biergarten was passing Delaware Avenue at 2:15 that morning, after leaving the home of Dr. Craig Gibson. And it was purely by coincidence, too—along with, perhaps, a sudden shift in the direction of the psychic breeze—that he looked to his left to see a young, brown-haired, shabbily dressed girl stumbling through the glow of a streetlight one hundred and fifty feet away.

He braked hard; the Woody pulled to the right; he swung a wide left onto Delaware Avenue and floored the accelerator. Beside him on the passenger's seat, Creosote whimpered in his sleep, as if in protest. Ryerson braked hard again so the Woody came to a halt beside the streetlamp. He jumped from the wagon, looked over its roof in the direction the girl had been moving, between two darkened houses, and called, "Hello. Are you there? Are you all right?"

He heard weeping at a distance, from that direction, and he strained to see past the glow of the streetlamp and into the area between the houses, but his eyesight was pitifully poor at night and he saw little more than the vague, hulking dark shapes of the houses, and a shaft of blacker darkness in between.

The weeping grew softer, as if the girl were moving away from him. "Hello?" he called again. "Are you all right? Answer me, please!" He hesitated going after her in the darkness. Six months earlier, near the end of his investigation of the murders in Rochester, New York, he'd gone after someone else in darkness and it had nearly cost him his life. He had, then, to rely on the sight of the creature he was chasing, to see through its eyes.

"Please!" he called now. "I want to help you."

The source of the weeping seemed to steady at a point midway between the houses. Ryerson saw a light go on in the second floor of the left-hand house; he heard a dog begin to bark somewhere far down the block. Then, screwing up courage against his night blindness, he walked out of the glow of the streetlamp and into the darkness.

A porchlight went on at the same house, the front door opened, and a thin woman in her fifties, dressed in a green nightgown and a man's dark suit coat, appeared in the doorway. "What's going on here?" she whispered harshly, as if afraid her own voice would wake the neighbors.

Ryerson, crossing her lawn, said, "There's someone in trouble," and nodded at the area between the houses. "There!"

"Trouble?" the woman said.

"Someone's hurt, I think," Ryerson added.

"Someone's hurt?" the woman said. "Who?"

Ryerson was parallel with the front of the house now. He said, as he vanished into the darkness at the side of the house, "I don't know."

The woman said, "I'm calling the police," and slammed her door shut. A moment later

Ryerson heard it being locked and bolted. Then he heard, in front of him, "I didn't mean it." It was the voice of a young girl.

He stopped. He could see nothing ahead of him in the area between the houses. He said, in his most soothing tones, "Please, come into the light."

"No," the girl said.

"Are you hurt?" Ryerson said.

"Yes," said the girl. "I'm hurt," and it was clear from her tone that she was telling the truth.

Ryerson took a couple of steps forward.

"Please," the girl said frantically, "stay where you are!"

"Yes," Ryerson said, "I will. I'm sorry." Then, for an instant, he got a picture of himself backlit by the light of the streetlamp a hundred feet behind him. He was seeing through the eyes of this young girl, he realized. A stab of pain shot through his belly; he winced. The pain dissipated. He said, "Where are you hurt? Is it your stomach?"

After a moment the girl answered, as if surprised, "Yes. It's my stomach. God, it hurts!"

Ryerson got an image of himself once again, through her eyes, and the image stayed with him long enough that he was able to gauge from it how far away he was from the girl—too far, he knew, to lunge for her, which would probably be foolish, anyway. He asked, "Are you carrying a weapon?" He wasn't sure why he'd asked it; it seemed a ludicrous question at best.

The girl said, "No. No."

He didn't believe her. As she spoke, the image of a gun settled coldly and suddenly into his head. And just as suddenly, he did not want at all to be there, in the darkness, where his eyes were useless. He said, voice quaking noticeably, "I want to help you; believe me, I want to help you. If you have . . ." Again a hot pain seared through his belly; again he winced and the pain was gone. He went on, voice quaking once more, as much now from sudden exhaustion as from fear—as if a kind of psychic adrenaline had pushed through him, leaving him light-headed and weak. "If you have a gun pointed at me, I would really appreciate it if you'd point it at something else."

She began to weep again.

And Ryerson realized his mistake. She did not have a gun pointed at him. "My God," he breathed, "you've been shot, haven't you?"

Then, mercifully, from behind him, on the street, he heard the wail of police sirens winding down and the screech of brakes. He glanced around. "Over here!" he called.

Buffalo's Tenth Precinct captain looked very skeptical. He was a balding, cigar-smoking bear of a man named Jack Lucas who was, Ryerson thought, the living amalgamation of all the hard-boiled, hard-bitten, but deep-down-soft-as-butter police captains that TV cop shows had ever produced. Ryerson thought, too, that the man had indeed developed much of his own tough but lovable persona from those same cop-show police captains. Lucas said, letting cigar smoke sift from his mouth as he spoke, "And you say that you're a *psychic*, Mr. Biergarten?"

Ryerson, the sleeping Creosote in his lap, nodded. "Yes, sir. Actually, I'm a psychic investigator." He was surprised, even a little disappointed, though he'd never have admitted it, that the man hadn't heard of him. He added, "As a matter of fact, I've helped a few police departments from time to time—"

Lucas cut in, "Then they're assholes, Mr. Biergarten, because I don't believe in any of that crap. Everything's got a logical explanation, everything's explainable, everything's real; if you can't touch it or smell it or taste it or fuck it, then by God it doesn't exist!"

Ryerson shrugged, "Yes, I agree, but—"

"How well do you know this girl, this"—he leaned forward, checked the police report on his desk—"this Laurie Drake, Mr. Biergarten?"

Sensing trouble, Ryerson answered, "I *don't* know her, Captain Lucas. That's the first time I've heard her name, in fact."

Lucas leaned back in his oak desk chair and nodded slowly. "Uh-huh," he sneered, "and my granny eats horseshit for breakfast."

Ryerson found himself getting angry. He didn't want to get angry, because when he got angry his psychic ability either shut down altogether or it went haywire. Here, he guessed—in the Homicide Division of the Buffalo Police Department—it would go haywire. The potential flood of input was simply too great, the psychic atmosphere too much in turmoil; he could see himself fighting very hard to look like something more than a madman. It had happened before, at theaters and shopping malls, and, for some strange and obscure reason, at post offices. He usually won the fight to present an appearance of normalcy, though it left him exhausted for hours. He said tightly, "If there's some charge you want to place against me—"

Again, Captain Lucas interrupted him. "What are we going to charge you with, Mr. Biergarten? Do you have anything in mind? You've been very helpful to us. She was a fugitive, you know. This"—again he checked the police report—"this Laurie Drake. She was a fugitive and you helped us catch her. My God, we should be giving you a commendation, shouldn't we? We should be giving you the key to the fucking city, shouldn't we? So tell me, why do you want us to *charge* you with something? And why in God's name am I so damned inclined to do it?" He stopped, clearly for effect.

But Ryerson jumped into the gap. "You damned cretin!" he snarled. "I have no more to do with that poor girl than your dung-eating granny does. Now I will repeat, unless you have a specific charge to place against me, I'll accept your thanks and go back to my motel room."

A long, slow, angry grin spread over Lucas's mouth. He leaned forward, put his elbows on his cluttered desk, and, still grinning, popped his cigar into his mouth and rolled it from one side to the other. "Why did you come to Buffalo, Mr. Biergarten?"

Ryerson answered, "That's none of your business."

"I can *make* it my business."

Ryerson pushed himself abruptly to his feet. "Then do it!" he hissed, and turned to go. A detective appeared at the open door. "Captain Lucas?" he said.

"Yeah," Lucas growled, "what is it, Spurling?"

Spurling said, "They dug the bullet out of that girl's stomach. It's from someone's service revolver, sir."

A name came to Ryerson. It came to him quickly, and there was pain attached to it. And, had he been thinking—had he been *able* to think beneath the psychic storm that was raging inside his head—he'd have stayed quiet. But, like a burp, the name "Newman" escaped him, and, sighing, he wished to heaven that he could snatch it back; he even thought for one glorious moment that neither Spurling nor Lucas had heard him.

But Spurling was looking wide-eyed at him in astonishment.

And behind him Lucas jumped to his feet and barked, "Get me Gail Newman's address and phone number. Then book this asshole!"

Leonard McGuire, Uniformed Officer, Buffalo Police Department

All his life, Leonard McGuire wanted only to be of service, wanted only to do what he was told to do because that made life easier for him. At home, his father—who had assured him time and again that he, Leonard, "didn't have the brains that God gave geese"—made all of Leonard's decisions for him, because, he assured Leonard, "You certainly can't make them yourself." In school, Leonard, who was not at all stupid, did precisely what he was told by his teachers and made it through twelve grades with hassles to no one. When he joined the Marines, he was sure that most decisions would be made for him, decisions like when to get up, when and how to eat, when and how to take showers, when, even, to go and find a woman to spend time with. And for a while in boot camp it was true; all his decisions were made for him and he was as contented as a sleeping cat in a pocket of sunlight. But then boot camp ended, he was shipped off to be an electrician's mate aboard an aircraft carrier, and for the first time in his life he was required to make his own decisions. And because he never had, he couldn't. He buckled, snapped, and was discharged. Several years later he was hired by the Buffalo Police Department (thanks to the fact that his father was then a city councilman). His solemn and secret vow was this; never make waves, never seek promotion, do what you are told, do it immediately, enforce the law, be invisible. He thought he had the tools to do this. He thought his career with the Buffalo Police Department was going to be long and peaceful. But soon he found that decisions were required of him every day—*Do I let this speeder go with only a warning? Do I draw my gun on this guy whose hand is so close to a knife? Do I pick up that streetwalker or wait for someone from Vice to do it? Do I look the other way when I see someone take two or three newspapers from the automatic vendor on the corner?* These questions were tough questions at first. After all, hadn't he been assured over and over again that he didn't have the ability to make his own decisions? Hadn't someone always made decisions for him?

But much to his surprise, he found that he could make decisions, that his mental apparatus was in pretty good working order, in fact. When, for instance, the streetwalker sauntered up to someone's car and leaned over, he knew that all he had to do was cruise by, maybe say, "Take it somewhere else, honey," because it was a victimless crime, after all, and it was Vice's job to regulate it. And so he began to make decisions. Most of them were right; some of them weren't. And after a while the ones that weren't began to turn the tide, began to convince him yet again that, as his father had said, he didn't have the brains that God gave geese. Then each of his decisions became momentous and nerve-jarring. And he longed to have all those decisions made for him, so when he was wrong, someone else would get the blame.

In "The District"

He couldn't believe it, but it was true. At last he had forgotten his name. He smiled at that. It was funny forgetting his name. It was something to laugh about. But he didn't laugh; he hadn't laughed, he guessed, in ten years. He only smiled, took another slug of MD 20/20, and put the bottle on the pavement between his legs. He sensed that one of the thousands of rats that roamed this area was nosing about nearby, so he waved weakly at it, mumbled, "Go way, get outa here!" then picked up the bottle again. He turned his head in the direction of the rat, which was scurrying off into the darkness. "You'll have your chance quick enough!"

John, he thought. Sure, that was his name. Or *George*. Or *Bill*. It was something common, anyway.

To his right, he saw the headlights of a car approaching. He lifted his hand to shield his eyes from the glare, muttered a curse. Moments later the car pulled up on the wrong side of the road, so the driver's side was directly in front of him. The window went down. He heard: "Whatcha doin' there, buddy?"

He answered, "I'm dyin' here. What's it to ya?"

The driver chuckled. "That sounds like a hell of a way to spend an evening. Why don't you hop in, and I'll drive you down to the Salvation Army for the night."

"No thanks. I don't like it there. They make you pray."

"Nothing wrong with prayer, my friend."

"Didn't say there was."

Another chuckle, then the driver's voice grew tighter, more demanding. "Why don't you get in the car anyway?"

"An' why don'tchoo get fucked!"

The driver's door flew open. Moments later, John, or George, or Bill, found himself being thrown into the car's backseat and heading south down Peacock Street. He mumbled a few incoherent curses, vomited, then passed out.

When he awoke thirty minutes later, he had a scant three minutes to live.

They were the most pleasurable three minutes of his life.

Chapter Ten

The trick that Joan Mott Evans used to rouse herself from sleep when the dream began was a simple one. When she saw that she was approaching the spot where Lila was buried—and she always approached it from the east, through a field of horsetail and clover, at night, under a full moon—she bit her lip very hard, hard enough, in fact, that when she awoke, she found that she was bleeding. But that was okay—the blood was okay. Because the dream was hell.

It's what she did the night that Ryerson Biergarten was doing his clumsy dance for Captain Jack Lucas. She came up over the rise in the field of horsetail and clover—it had the creamy sheen of a full moon on it. She saw the wire fence to her left, used to keep the horses that once roamed these fields from wandering into the roadway. She saw, at the bottom of the slope, the place where Lila Curtis was buried. And she knew that the nightmare was about to begin again.

So she bit her lip. And started the blood. And awoke screaming, "Lila, I'm sorry, I'm so sorry!" Then, because it was a scene that had been repeated countless times in the past four months, the panic, the fear, and the enormous sense of pleading and apology wore away almost at once, and she was left to get out of bed and take a long, hot shower to wash the sweat off.

The first words Gail Newman said when her eyes fluttered open and she saw Guy Mallory's face above her were, "How is she? How's Laurie?"

Mallory, who wanted very much to be tough about it, who wanted to growl at her, "She's locked up, thank God," saw that Gail was genuinely concerned, so he answered simply, "She's going to be okay. They got the bullet out and she's going to be okay."

Gail's eyes closed. "Thank God," she whispered. She could feel the starched sheets beneath her, could smell the faint sting of antiseptic, could hear someone being paged once, then again, over the hospital intercom. She whispered, "I had to do it, Guy. I had no choice. She came after me." She opened her eyes again. "I really had to do it!" she insisted, her voice high and hard and tense because she'd mistaken the look of concern on Guy's face for one of skepticism.

He nodded once. "Yes, I know."

Gail became aware of the bandage around her neck, and of the IV letting blood into her arm. She asked confusedly, "What'd she do to me, Guy?"

Guy answered, a small nervous smile flitting across his mouth, "She bit you. As close as we can tell, she bit you, Gail." He hesitated, as if uncertain how to continue.

"And?" Gail coaxed.

He shrugged. "I don't know, sweet cheeks. They tell me you lost a lot of blood." He inhaled deeply, was clearly finding it hard to continue.

Gail coaxed again, "C'mon, Guy, be straight with me, okay?"

She saw another nervous smile appear on his mouth, saw him glance around. "Oh, hi," he said.

Another male face appeared next to his—the face of a man in his sturdy sixties who had a full head of bright white hair, piercing hazel eyes, and an air of quiet but intense authority about him. "Hello, Miss Newman," he said. "I'm Dr. Chandler; I'd like to ask you a question or two if you feel up to it."

"What the *hell* is going on here?!" Gail said aloud, and felt a sudden wave of nausea and dizziness wash over her.

Guy began, "She bit you, Gail, like I said—"

And Dr. Chandler broke in. "Sergeant Mallory, if you could please leave me alone with Miss Newman for a few minutes."

Guy shrugged, said, "Sure okay, I'll be right out here," and left the room.

Chandler began, summoning up a kind of stiff and uneasy bedside manner, "So tell me how you're feeling, Miss Newman; you gave us all a bit of a scare."

Gail said, "What did she do to me, Doctor?"

Dr. Chandler appeared to be considering her question for a moment. Then he nodded. "As the sergeant said, Miss Newman, you were bitten—"

"For Christ's sake, how many times do I have to be *told* that?" She stopped, again felt nauseous, closed her eyes against it.

"Dizzy?" Chandler asked.

She nodded.

"You lost a good bit of blood, I'm afraid," he added.

Gail whispered tightly, "She bit me, I *know* that, Doctor. But for God's sake, what *else* did she do?"

"Yes," he said, clearly to gain time. After a moment he went on. "Actually, we think she ... withdrew some of your blood—"

"Oh my God!"

"A small amount—"

"She *sucked* my blood?!" Gail cut in. "My God, what does she think she is, some kind of vampire?" Again, dizziness pushed through her. She closed her eyes.

And Chandler said, "Yes. I'm afraid that's precisely what she thinks."

"Wait a minute," Irene in the Records Division said to her coworker, Glen Coffman, "*I* remember someone named Curtis."

Glen growled at her, his fingers poised over his keyboard, gaze fixed on his computer monitor. "In a moment, Irene; I've got Darth Vader cornered here!"

She looked at him, astonished. "Glen, this is not a video arcade!"

"We all need a diversion, Irene." He punched three keys in rapid succession, then threw himself back angrily in his gray metal secretarial chair. "Dammit, goddammit!" he hissed. "I almost had him!"

"Can you forget about Darth Vader for a moment, Glen? I'm trying to talk to you about this file I've been trying to open for the last five days."

He sighed, got up, went over, studied her screen. It read, as before:

FILE DIRECTORY
CURTIS L.BAK	JME.BAK	HAWKINS.LET	LET.BAK
FORMAT.CMD	STAT.CMD	OPER.CMD	JME.OPE

USER NUMBER?

He shrugged. "I see you still haven't opened it." A pause. "You want my advice, Irene? Give it up. If there are no hard copies available anywhere, it's clearly something of no interest to the Buffalo Police Department."

She sighed. "We won't know *that* until we get a look at it, will we, Glen?"

Another shrug. "Okay, so don't take my advice."

"Gladly. I only wanted you to know that I think I remember someone named Curtis."

"So do I," Glen offered. "She was my kindergarten teacher. Miss Curtis. Great big fat woman; she had a mustache and smelled like sour cream."

Irene sighed again. "Can you be serious for just half a minute, Glen?"

"Sure." He checked his watch. "Starting now."

'Thanks."

"So?" he coaxed.

"So, I was only saying that I remember someone named Curtis. I remember it was a case from outside Buffalo, outside New York, in fact, if I'm not mistaken." She paused.

"And?"

"And that's about it. It was a murder case, I think. A murder/suicide—"

Glen was nodding.

"Why are you nodding?" Irene asked.

"I remember it, too. Her name was Lilian or Lily—something. But her last name was Curtis, and you're right, it was a murder/suicide; I remember reading about it in the *Evening News*, maybe four, five months ago. It was a story out of Pennsylvania, I think."

Irene stood. "I'll be back in a while."

"Where you going?"

"To the *Evening News*. I'm going to check their morgue."

Glen looked at his watch again. "Irene, it's ten-thirty; their morgue's not open now."

She started for the door. "It is for people whose boyfriends are city editors."

"Oh," he nodded. "Yes, I see."

Detective Spurling and Captain Lucas booked Ryerson as a material witness in a case of attempted murder. It landed him in the Buffalo jail for the night, *sans* Creosote, who was given over to a police matron. "I hate these snotty little dogs," she explained, but agreed to keep him until morning when, Ryerson presumed, he'd be able to post bail.

He was in something of a blue funk, because while he hated jails, as everyone did, added to the usual reasons (they were places where people were locked up; they smelled bad; the people in them were almost universally unpleasant) was the fact that the psychic input here was not only dizzying and overwhelming, as it was in shopping malls and post offices, it was depressing as hell, too. It was sepia-toned, dead-ended, and desperate in a futile and resigned way. In his head it looked the way it smelled—of urine, sweat, and stale cigarette smoke.

So, the blue funk persisted.

It wasn't the first time he'd been in jail. During his junior year at Duke University he'd gotten rip-roaring drunk with several other juniors and they had collectively mooned the sorority house where Coreen lived. They were caught, as the cop who arrested them said, "with their pants down," charged with "lewd and lascivious behavior" and put in the drunk tank for the night.

It wasn't the last time Ryerson got drunk. For five years after that he consistently worked himself into a stupor, consistently made a fool of himself in public places, and consistently got arrested. At last, he realized that he was sliding into alcoholism, and that if he didn't quit drinking, he'd slowly kill himself. A year later, after several failed attempts at putting booze behind him, he was offered a drink and said no. On the night that he sat in a blue funk in the Buffalo holding cell, he hadn't had a drink in nearly fifteen years.

In "The District"

"Power!" the woman breathed. She had *power*. Power to *be*, to *have*, to *control*, power to *change*! It made up for the darkness, made up for the pain, made up for her time here in this damp and stinking place.

Because another damp and stinking place was where she had sprung up and had begun to visit herself upon the earth.

Power! Control! Change!

And what had that last poor fool called her—*werewolf*? That was for others to imagine, only one of the evil fantasies her beautiful living children could indulge in and so, through it, take power for themselves.

And so give power to her.

Werewolf indeed! The fool. That was for that other creature. The creature she had sprung from. The creature whose flesh hung now like paper on its bones and whose eyes mingled with the liquid that its brain had become.

Captain Lucas came to Ryerson's cell at 9:30 that morning. He had a sheet from a computer printout in his hand, and as the guard opened the cell door for him, he smiled gloatingly.

He sat on the bed next to Ryerson and held up the sheet of paper as if holding up a picture of one of his kids; "You know what this is, Dr. Biergarten?"

Ryerson glanced disinterestedly at him, and looked away. "I don't like to be called doctor."

"Shit," Lucas cried, "I would if I were you. If I had a fucking doctorate in *para*psychology, I'd sure as hell want to be called fucking doctor."

Ryerson shrugged. "Call me what you wish to call me."

Lucas guffawed. "Call you anything but sober, isn't that right?" He guffawed again, immensely pleased with his joke.

Ryerson chose to ignore the remark; he

nodded at the computer printout. "What you have there, Captain Lucas, is a litany of past mistakes. I paid for those mistakes, and I can't see that what happened a decade and a half ago has any bearing at all on what you're investigating now."

It was Lucas's turn to shrug. "What we have here, Dr. Biergarten, is the record of a loser. Once an alky, always an alky, that's what I say."

"You're a real phrasemaker, aren't you, Captain?"

Lucas quickly grew angry. He waved the computer printout so it flapped in the air. "Whether this has anything to do with Laurie Drake and Detective Newman is something we have yet to determine—"

Ryerson cut in, sighing. "You called Tom McCabe, didn't you?" Tom McCabe was Chief of Detectives in Rochester, New York, where Ryerson had worked on what had become known as "the park werewolf." He and McCabe had grown close during his investigation, and Ryerson assumed he'd be an excellent character reference.

Lucas said, "Yeah. Sure. I called him. How'd *you* know?"

Ryerson answered simply, "I know a lot of things, Captain." He paused. "I assume that Tom vouched for me?"

"He said you worked with him and he said he was sorry to hear you were in trouble. That's about it."

"You're lying."

Captain Lucas grinned. "What*ever* your friend said, Mr. Biergarten, doesn't make a bit of difference here. I don't care if you're the fucking queen of France, you're trying to play footsy with us and I don't like it one damn bit."

Ryerson leveled a withering gaze at him; he wished mightily that his gifts included telekinesis as well, so he could mentally untie the man's shoelaces or make his cigar fall into his lap. Instead, he said, "Tell me, Captain Lucas—just how much do you value your credibility here at the Buffalo Police Department?"

Lucas looked confused, a little apprehensive. "What are you talking about?"

Ryerson shrugged; he hated doing this, he thought a person's private life should indeed remain private, but for some reason this man bore him a lot of animosity, and if the man had his way, Ryerson would probably sit in the holding cell until Christmas. He said, "What I'm talking about, Captain, is what you do at night. At"—he paused, probed about in the psychic atmosphere—"at Ed's Place."

Lucas grinned broadly. "Ain't no Ed's Place in Buffalo, my friend." He put his hands palm down on the bed, as if preparing to stand.

Ryerson went on. "The name of the place doesn't matter much. Whatever it's called, it's what you do there that gives you such a kick, isn't it?"

Lucas hissed, "You son of a bitch!"

Ryerson shook his head. "No, Captain. I just want to get out of here, that's all. And if I have to blackmail you to do it, then I will."

Lucas's cheeks puffed several times with anger and frustration. Finally, he pushed himself violently to his feet, went to the cell door, barked, "Guard! Guard!" glanced around at Ryerson, and said very succinctly—through lips tightly clenched with anger—"You'll be free as soon as I can clear the paperwork. Just don't leave the city."

"I have no intention of leaving the city," Ryerson said. "I've got business to attend to here."

Then the guard came and let the captain out.

Ryerson sighed. He thought that the years he'd spent gambling—which seemed to have gone hand in hand with his drinking—had paid off; at least he'd learned how to bluff. Because what he'd read from Captain Lucas had merely been vague—only that Lucas went to a bar on certain nights and while he was there he did something that made him feel ashamed. Ryerson had read no more than that. He didn't think he'd have been able to, anyway, because whatever it was that Lucas did at the bar made him feel so very ashamed that he pushed it far back into his consciousness and let it lie hidden most of the time.

At 11:00 that morning Ryerson was let out of the holding cell. He located the police matron—who was getting ready to go home—got Creosote back, was told by the desk sergeant that the Woody was at the Buffalo Impound Garage, five blocks away, and was reminded one more time by a growling Captain Lucas, "I don't care what you *think* you know about me, ace; if you try to go back to Boston or whatever damned hole you climbed out of, I'll haul your bare ass back here personally."

It was 11:25 A.M. when Lucas gave Ryerson this warning.

Not quite five minutes later Laurie Drake, in Room 12 of the hospital wing of the Buffalo City Jail, began to suffer the torments of the damned.

The thing inside Laurie had no color, or shape, or smell, but it did have mass, though very little of it, and weight, about a quarter of a gram, and it traveled about in her veins like a blood clot. Most of the time in the past two months, ever since, on a dare, she'd gone at night into the area called "The District," she had had no idea she was playing host to it; she'd felt a vague discomfort now and again, or her belly ached, and she would think that she was at last beginning to have her period.

And when the change started, pretty, laughing, "academically talented" Laurie Drake was all but squashed by the entity of her own creation. Laurie Drake—who secretly longed for the mama doll she'd carted through infancy and into preadolescence and had at last thrown away to prove she was indeed growing up—was squashed by the tall, buxom, incredibly sensual and murderous woman that lived deep inside her adolescent fantasies. The fantasy she had built up out of a character in a movie.

The thing inside her fed on the darkness in that fantasy. It saw *murder* there, and built on it; it saw *hunger* there, and built on it. It changed Laurie Drake inexorably. It changed her into the fantasy that lived and moved at first only inside her head.

And then it made that fantasy into something sensuously and murderously real.

In Room 12 of the hospital wing of the Buffalo City Jail, Laurie Drake again began to change.

But she didn't want to change.

She wanted to stay what she was—the pretty, brown-haired, twelve-year-old girl who secretly longed for her mama doll. She was tired of being squashed, buried, pushed back.

And so she fought the change. And it fought her.

And the pain therefore was incredible.

Chapter Eleven

The nurse on duty was drinking apple juice. It was lunchtime, and because she was a very health-conscious person, she'd brought a very healthful lunch—a quart of apple juice to keep her regular, sprout sandwiches made with nine-grain bread for iron and protein and B vitamins, and a crunchy granola bar for dessert.

The nurse's name was Tabby (short for Tabitha) Makepeace. She was thirty-one years old, firm of body and mind, and at the moment that she heard the scream from Room 12, she was smiling pleasantly and thinking that her dog really should be getting more bone meal.

She was also in the middle of a long tug on the quart container of apple juice when she heard the scream from Room 12, and the muscle spasm that racked her body made her throat close up, so what was at the top half of her throat got spit out, and what was at the bottom half went down the wrong pipe.

Fully half a minute later, when her gagging and gasping for air had subsided to occasional coughs, she heard another scream, just as loud, and just as pain-ridden as the first. She whispered, "Oh Jesus Lord God in Heaven," jumped to her feet, and moved as fast as her very healthy legs could carry her to Room 12.

And wanted, as soon as she threw the door open and saw what was in the room, to stop and run screaming in the other direction. But because her emotional and physical momentum were simply too great, she half-stumbled, half-ran partway into the room and was there pulled firmly, lovingly, hungrily into the arms of a tall, buxom, and incredibly sensuous woman. And the life was sucked noisily out of her within minutes.

Access to the hospital wing of the Buffalo City Jail was gained through a set of sliding barred doors about thirty feet east of Tabby's station. Sitting near these barred doors was an aging, disease-ridden cop named George Orlando who was, at the time of Tabby's murder, absorbed in the latest issue of the survivalist magazine *Exotic Weaponry*: smack dab in the middle of the cover there was an ad for the magazine's newest bumper sticker;

the bumper sticker read, KILL A COMMIE FOR MOMMY. That tickled George because he'd done a lot of commie killing during the Korean War, and they had been the best years of his life.

Covering the barred doors that let people in and out of the hospital wing, there was a layer of thick, unbreakable glass. This was why George hadn't heard the first screams from Room 12, or the abrupt scream from Tabby Makepeace when the life was sucked from her.

So George, absorbed in his copy of *Exotic Weaponry*, heard absolutely nothing. Had he been twenty years younger, and his hearing more acute, he would have heard a set of small, shrill, hollow noises that might have gotten his momentary attention.

Besides being racked by various diseases— one was a lingering low-grade hepatitis, still another was psoriasis—George was incredibly nearsighted. Recently, the powers that be had discussed asking him to resign voluntarily because he was in such lousy shape, but it was decided that for the two years remaining until his twenty-five-year retirement, sitting guard at the hospital wing probably wouldn't get him into too much trouble.

So, because he was nearsighted, what he saw when he looked up after sensing movement down the corridor, beyond the glassed and barred doors, was a vague but very suggestive form moving toward him, as if he were looking at a naked woman through a wet, translucent shower curtain.

He stood from his metal stool, a lascivious grin played on his mouth, and he rubbed his eyes hard as if that would help him to see better. And, as a matter of fact, it did, if just briefly, just long enough for him to see that what was moving toward him down the corridor was indeed a naked woman. And had he, for that brief moment, focused on the woman's face instead of on her incredible body, he would have seen that blood ringed her mouth, a mouth that was open wide to reveal the inch-long canines gleaming dully within.

But, too soon, she was behind the wet, translucent curtain again. And what he saw of her mouth then convinced him only that she was wearing too much dull red lipstick.

She got to the barred door, pressed her nakedness into it, and clawed screechingly at the glass with her fingernails. George's fantasies gave him no choice but to press the button that opened the door and let her spill out over him, onto him, and push those awful canines into his thick grayish-pink neck while he grinned broadly, and loud nasal *"uhnns"* of pleasure came from him. Until he died.

Joan Mott Evans felt ill at ease. She thought her mother, rest her soul, would have said, "Someone's walking over your grave, Joanie," a phrase that much appealed to Joan because of its commingling of various apparent absurdities (time as a kind of Möbius band that's constantly folding back on itself; death as a state of continuous static wakefulness; resurrection as a small whispered promise). She thought it was likely that someone she didn't want to see was going to visit her that day. Similar ideas had proved correct in the past. Like the time her former sister-in-law, Judith, a woman who was obsessed with money-making plans for the housewife—Amway, Tupperware, envelope-stuffing, et cetera—had shown up with all her paraphernalia in hand, brought it into Joan's house, dumped it in the garbage, and announced, "I'm going to save you," because, she explained, she had given up making money in favor of, as she'd put it coyly, "making time with Jesus, instead." Joan had had an out that day. She was on her way to visit Lila Curtis, her new young friend who lived in Edgewater, just twenty miles south of Erie, where she had lived at the time. Lila had to take her driving test and Joan had offered her car to take it in; so Judith, smiling a promise that she would be back, left the house.

Minutes later, so did Joan. She drove to Edgewater, pulled up in front of Lila's house, honked the horn. She knew then that she should probably go inside and chat with Lila's parents. How did it look, after all, to have their sixteen-year-old daughter honked for by a twenty-three-year-old woman who claimed merely to be their daughter's friend? But she didn't like Lila's parents. They were cloying and possessive and judgmental. She could read it in them, in the aura they projected, more than in anything they said or did. She thought that Mr. Curtis, for instance, had ideas about his daughter that bordered on the unhealthy. And she thought that Mrs. Curtis knew this and blamed Lila for it. Caught in the middle, of course, was poor Lila—a good-natured, artistic, joke-telling girl who seemed to have struggled heroically out of her parents' bizarre attitudes toward her and developed a winning personality all her own.

But that day, the day of her driving test, Joan knew that something was wrong as soon as Lila got into the car. She could see trouble in her, in her eyes and in the set of her mouth. And every once in a while something tight and cold and miserable leaped from Lila's brain into hers and made her shiver.

"What's wrong?" Joan asked.

And Lila, flashing a pale copy of her usual bright smile, answered, "Just nervous. About the test."

Joan nodded. "Sure. That's understandable, but you've been driving now for three or four months. Just pretend when the examiner sits down there"—she nodded at Lila's side of the seat—"that it's me."

Lila's smile flattened. "Thanks. That's a good idea. I'll do it."

Joan studied her for a few seconds. "What's wrong, Lila?"

Lila, looking straight ahead, answered, "I'm sick, Joan. Oh, God, I'm so sick!"

That had been the beginning of their walk together through hell.

Now, seven months later, after Joan's ill-at-ease feeling had dissipated, there was a soft knock at her front door. She got a twinge of apprehension, no more, then, convincing herself that it was only the paper boy collecting, she went and answered the knock.

Her face dropped when she saw Ryerson Biergarten, Creosote in his arms, standing on the porch. He smiled apologetically. "Am I disturbing you, Joan?"

"Of course you are," she answered, pretending weariness.

His smile faded. "We've got to talk, Joan," he said. "About Lila."

She sighed resignedly, because she'd heard a very firm resolve in his voice. She nodded. "Yes. We do," she said, and backed away from the door to let him into the house.

At the Buffalo Police Department's Records Division

Glen Coffman asked, "What'd you find out at the *Evening News* last night, Irene?"

She punched a few figures onto an equation she was jumbling, glanced at him. "Nothing. They wouldn't let me in."

Glen smiled, pleased. "Didn't you tell them who you were?"

"Of course I told them who I was. I told them I was a cop, and they—"

"Wait. Who's 'they'?"

"A janitor."

"Oh."

"A wise-ass janitor at that, too. He said if I wanted to get into the building's morgue at that hour, I had to have a warrant. Jesus, everyone's a damned civil libertarian." She sighed. "And I guess there's nothing wrong with that, really. It's just that I hate wasting my time."

"What about your boyfriend?"

"What about him? He wasn't there."

"Didn't the janitor know him?" Glen was smiling; he was clearly enjoying himself.

Irene looked askance at him. "Why don't you get out your Space Wars or your Star Wars or whatever juvenile game you play when you should be working?"

"Don't mind if I do." A pause. "You going back there today, Irene?"

"Yes," she answered.

Chapter Twelve

The woman was sated. And because she was sated, and Laurie's fantasy satisfied, and the incredible need gone, if just temporarily—like the feeling of release that comes after orgasm—Laurie herself should have by now made a reappearance.

But she hadn't.

She lay inside the woman, beaten and weary from battle with her, unable even to cry out again, "Mommy. Help me, Mommy!" She wanted only to fall into a long and dreamless sleep, where she did not have to be a part of this woman, where she did not have to watch the woman animate herself so sensuously and murderously; where she did not have to hear the awful sucking sounds and feel the warm blood coursing into her mouth, and into her throat, and into her belly.

The belly where Gail Newman's bullet had been.

The belly that was torn and bleeding now because of this woman. The belly that threatened to split open and end both their lives.

But there was this, too: The woman had begun to think, to reason. She had changed—because Laurie's fantasies about her had changed—from what had at first been merely an overripe eating machine, to vampire, and now into a sentient being, who, at any moment, could toss the bleeding, dying Laurie Drake inside her away, like some kind of tumor, and go off—a new and separate creature from her host—to do the things that her host's fantasies had told her she must do.

She was wearing clothes that she'd found in the Buffalo City Jail's locker room, a blessedly short distance from where she'd encountered George Orlando, and where his body now lay, a fearsome smile on his face. The clothes were a size smaller than her body required, but that was okay; tight was appealing. She was wearing a long-sleeved white blouse, no bra, a green cardigan sweater that barely took the chill off the early November day, a black, mid-calf-length form-fitting skirt, and red high heels. She was a quarter mile east of the jail, on Lawrence Street, in a fashionable and self-important neighborhood of small elite restaurants, and specialty shops—a yuppie's paradise. Around her, men of various ages, and even a few women, turned their heads to stare appreciatively, and she gave some of the men and some of the women a flat, close-mouthed, come-hither smile.

She did not dare open her mouth too wide, of course. As it was, the long, deadly canines within pushed into her lower gums slightly, making it appear, to the casual observer, that she was pouting.

"Hi, Alex?" she heard.

She turned her head to the left and saw a tall, thin, ruggedly handsome man dressed in a blue Chevron mechanic's uniform and matching hat. The man was bending over the open hood of a BMW 320i while the man in the driver's seat read a copy of *Fortune* magazine in the driver's seat.

The woman stopped walking and gave the mechanic her flat come-hither smile. She opened her mouth slightly. "Alex?" she said, her voice the same velvet drizzle it had been at John and Vera Brownleigh's house three nights earlier.

The man dropped a screw into place on the BMW's carburetor. "You don't remember me, do you?"

"Of course I do," the woman answered, still opening her mouth only a little; she knew instinctively the best answers to give her prey.

"I thought so," the man said. "How could you forget old Jimmy Buck, right?" He tightened the screw, fished another one from a spot in front of the radiator, dropped it into place. He was very good at his work, and it showed in the quick, efficient, graceful way he did it.

"I couldn't," the woman breathed.

And something suspicious passed across the man's brow because he'd just realized that this woman was not the woman he'd been with. "Yeah," he said, "good seeing you." He tightened the screw. "Start 'er up," he yelled, and the thirtyish yuppie male in the driver's seat started the BMW, smiled, and craned his well-coiffed head out the window. "What was the problem, Jimmy?"

"Stuck metering valve," Jimmy answered, and closed the hood. He turned to the woman on the sidewalk. He said, having decided at last that she was merely a hooker out of her usual territory, "Go on home, honey. These people don't want nothin' to do with the likes of you."

She said, pretending offense, "Why don't we let *them* be the judge of that."

The man in the BMW leaned over toward the driver's window and called in his most casual and unassuming voice—as if he merely wanted to do her a favor—"Going anywhere in particular, miss?"

"You believe in possession," Joan Mott Evans said.

Ryerson Biergarten, Creosote running about

near his feet, a soft plastic duck tightly clenched in his teeth, said, "We're all possessed by one thing or another. With some of us it's by our work. With others it's by alcohol or drugs. Why can't a very few of us be possessed by things we don't normally see or touch?" It was the paraphrase of a speech he used to give at his night class in parapsychology at New York University. He felt vaguely foolish and embarrassed now because he thought he sounded stiff and formal, which was precisely the opposite tone that he wanted to strike with this woman. Joan picked up on his embarrassment and decided to let him stew in it for a while. So there was silence for a few moments while Ryerson squirmed a bit, then Joan said, "Possession like in *The Exorcist*, you mean?"

Ryerson was across from her at her small kitchen table. He asked, "Do you believe in demons, Joan?"

"Yes," she answered at once with a firmness that surprised him. "Yes," she said again.

And he, making a guess based on what he was reading from her, asked, "Because of Lila?"

"No," she answered. "You said it yourself, Mr. Biergarten—"

"Rye, please."

"You said it yourself; I have 'the gift,' just like you. So, yes, I know there are demons, not because of Lila, but because I've *seen* them." She was very uncomfortable, though she tried valiantly to hide it.

Creosote abandoned the soft plastic duck in favor of one of Ryerson's argyle socks—he had a firm, growling bite on it that threatened to tear it from Ryerson's foot. Ryerson bent over, grabbed Creosote by the scruff of the neck with one hand, by the muzzle with the other, and pried the dog's jaws apart. Then he lifted the dog into his lap, looked him squarely in the eye, and said very firmly, pointing a stiff finger at him, "No! Bad dog!"

Joan said, "He doesn't know what you're talking about."

Ryerson looked offended. "Sure he does. I *know* he does."

Joan shrugged. "Okay, but my experience has been that you've got to *show* a dog what you're talking about, Rye. Mr. Biergarten," she corrected herself. "As far as he's concerned, all you're telling him is not to sit in your lap."

"Oh, come on. He's not *that* stupid!"

"Well, he's not human, is he? He's a dog. And dogs are basically dumb."

Ryerson grinned secretively. He could feel that Joan was loosening up. "What sort of demons do you see, Joan?"

Joan said, surprising him again, "No. I don't want to talk about that. I want to talk about dogs right now." It was a statement that could easily have sounded petulant, but didn't; it was merely a statement of fact. "We'll slide back into the subject of demons in a few minutes."

Ryerson grinned. "Sure," he said.

She said, "And I've got to tell you that whatever gifts you might have, Rye, a working knowledge of dogs is not high on the list."

The male yuppie, whose name was Alan Pierce, had what he called a "run-to" apartment on Lawrence Street. "You know," he explained, "a place to *run to* when the world is closing in on me, when the *house* is closing in on me, when *keeping up* is closing in on me," all the while smiling his sad, world-weary smile. "My wife has one, too. We have an interesting arrangement, my wife and I." And his world-weary smile altered slightly so it was a worldly-wise smile. "She takes her pleasure where she can, and I take mine where I can, but we reserve our greatest pleasure—giving and taking—for the times when we're together."

The woman with him, who had told him her name was Loni, was seated in one of his two red leather club chairs. She had her legs crossed fetchingly and was pretending to sip at a glass of Perrier he'd given her. She said, "I like that arrangement, Alan."

Alan was standing a few feet away, also with a glass of Perrier in hand. He was dressed in a pair of brown Haggar dress slacks with a knife-edged pleat, a blue striped button-down shirt, and tan RockSports. He had his right elbow cupped in his left palm so he could drink his Perrier without too many possibly clumsy movements, and he was trying very, very hard to make it appear that the sex he literally ached to get on with was of only passing importance to him; consequently, as he drank his Perrier, he looked as if he thought he might be wearing unmatched socks and didn't know how to check gracefully to see if he was or wasn't. He said, pausing in mid-sentence to sip the Perrier, "Pleasure is such a"—sip—"small part of life, isn't it, Loni?"

"No," she said. "It's really all there is to life, Alan."

He didn't know how to respond to that, though he agreed completely with it. He noticed, as possible witty/suggestive remarks passed through his head, that the left side of Loni's white blouse, at her rib cage, seemed to be fluttering slightly, as if a breeze were stirring it. He shifted his Perrier from one hand to the other, so his left elbow, now, was cupped in his right palm. "Life is what we make of it, isn't it, Loni?" he said. "Pleasure is what we make of life." It was a good turn of phrase, he thought.

She laughed despite herself, revealing for a moment the deadly canines. Alan didn't notice. His attention was again on the strange fluttering movements over her rib cage. Suddenly, she seemed to have lost a good bit of her amazing sexuality and was beginning to look bizarre, he thought. Even a little threatening. He said nervously, elbow moving about uncontrollably in his palm, the Perrier sloshing in the glass, "Is that funny?"

"What's funny?" she said. "You're funny."

A twisted nervous grin snaked about on his lips. "I don't mean to be," he said, and thought, *It's because I'm chunky. She's laughing at me because I'm chunky.* His attention riveted again on the fluttering movement over her rib cage. As he watched, it changed, grew more frantic; a lump appeared there, as if someone's head were trying to push through.

She laughed again, a high-pitched, squealing laugh that sounded like a siren out of control in a small, empty room.

Alan dropped his glass. It shattered on the hardwood floor; Perrier splattered all over the bottoms of his Haggar dress slacks and he glanced down and said, "Oh, shit!" He looked up again, at Loni. She was standing. Her mouth was open wide. And the lump at her rib cage was not a lump anymore. It was a basketball-sized mound that had ripped through the side of her blouse. He could see a few strands of gleaming wet brown hair there, at the head of the mound, and he could hear someone weeping and grunting intermittently as a soft, whitish-yellow substance like melted butter plopped to the floor around Loni's left side, below the bulge.

"Wanna mess around?" Loni said.

"No," Alan whispered, backing toward the door, his gaze flitting quickly from the mound as it grew larger, to Loni's face, and her marvelous gleaming canines. "Please, no. Thank you, no. I've got to be going, anyway; I've got to be going home to my wife; I'm sorry; she loves me and I love her; we love each other; love is all we have in life; I'm sorry . . ." He knew he was babbling. He knew he was going to die.

Loni advanced quickly on him, took his well-coiffed head in her graceful, strong hands, and sank her teeth deep into his jugular. The last thing he saw was that mound at her rib cage explode. He did not see Laurie Drake's body pop out. He did not see it fall with a bone-crushing thump to the floor. He did not see it curl into the fetal position, and stick its thumb into its mouth, and open its eyes wide.

"For instance," Joan Mott Evans was saying just then, five miles away, "what do you do when he . . . makes a mistake in the house?"

Ryerson answered proudly, "He doesn't make mistakes. He never has, not even when I first brought him home."

Joan raised an eyebrow. "Then he's one in a million."

"Yes, he is," Ryerson said, still with unmistakable pride.

Joan nodded to indicate Creosote, who was again on the floor and again showing an interest in Ryerson's argyle socks. "Some of the demons I've seen have a face like his, Rye."

Ryerson looked quizzically at her, unsure if she was joking with him. "Oh?" he said. "That must have been damned spooky."

Again Joan raised an eyebrow, thinking he was poking fun at her. "It was," she said. "It is."

Like all Boston bull terriers, Creosote had a flat face, large eyes that were vaguely cockeyed, a wide mouth that showed lots of gum, and nostrils that were pink and flaring. He also had the added charm of a large black wart just below his right eye. He was hungrily studying Ryerson's left sock.

Ryerson said, "You're not kidding, are you, Joan?"

She smiled uncomfortably. "Not about that, Rye."

Creosote latched onto the sock. Ryerson reached quickly down, pried the dog's jaws apart, put him on his lap, stroked him—which caused a kind of ragged purring sound to start in the dog's throat—and said to Joan, "Where do you think these demons come from?"

She answered slowly, thoughtfully, "Not hell. I don't believe in hell. I believe in suffering and loneliness and pain. I believe that they exist and that they torment us. I believe that demons can bring them to us." She paused. Ryerson could read confusion and frustration from her, as if she wanted very much to say precisely what she meant but realized that it was impossible. He left the silence alone. After a few moments she went on. "I don't know where they come from. I guess they come from the same place that all suffering and loneliness and pain come from. From us. From all of us."

"You sound awfully cynical about the human race, Joan," Ryerson said, regretting at once his vaguely preachy tone.

She shook her head. "No. I'm not. Along with the pain I know there's joy. I've experienced it. Everyone has; some of us more than others, of course." An image of someone Ryerson guessed was Lila Curtis leaped from Joan's mind to his. "Sometimes it's a sort of balancing act, isn't it, Rye? The joy and the pain. I think if you've got just a little bit of pain it can smother a lot of joy." She smiled quickly, as if embarrassed. "Like a toothache."

Ryerson said gently, "Tell me about Lila's pain, Joan."

Joan sighed. "Yes," she nodded firmly. "I want to. I need to."

Power! the woman whispered. Enough power to break away from this damp, stinking, dark place someday soon and walk among the living.

Because she'd have life in her, too. Because the young ones, the strong ones, the ones with life coursing through them, would feed her. And as their numbers grew from the few that were with her here, now, the awful stuff she had been built up from would change; and she would change. She would become what they were.

Life would push through her.

And the others, the weak ones, the ones with life only at the edges of their eyes, and within their groins, would sustain her for a time. And they were plentiful enough.

The man saw to that.

He loved her, he wanted her, he needed her. Most of all, he wanted to live, so he saw to it that the weak ones, the ones no one watched after and no one cared for, were abundantly supplied.

And because he gave her what she needed, she gave him what he needed.

She gave him herself.

Chapter Thirteen

Joan Mott Evans said, "I loved her. I loved Lila." She paused, on the verge of tears. "I've told you that, haven't I, Rye?"

Ryerson reached out and put his hand comfortingly on hers. "Don't worry about repeating yourself, Joan. Just tell me what you want to tell me."

She closed her eyes briefly, sighed. "It's like putting a puzzle together, Rye. But the puzzle's got too many pieces, and they're all the same color."

He patted her hand. "Yes. I understand."

She glanced at him, then down at the table. "Maybe you do. I hope so." A short pause. "I didn't kill her." She looked up at him entreatingly. "Did you think I killed her?"

"No. I never thought that."

She looked down at the table again and

said softly, "Lila killed herself. And her boyfriend. She knew that something was wrong inside her; she knew they'd gotten her."

"They?"

"The demons."

"Yes. Of course."

"You think I'm nuts, don't you?"

"No. I think you have good reasons for your beliefs. Many people believe in demons. I have a friend, a cop actually, who claims that there are demons who sit on his chest at night."

Joan looked offended. "Don't make fun of me, Rye."

He frowned. "I'm only trying to let you know that if you thought you were alone—"

"I never thought I was alone." It was a simple statement of fact. "Never alone. Only by myself from time to time. Like Lila."

"Are you saying there are similarities between you and Lila, Joan?"

She looked surprised by the question. "Of course there are. We're both vulnerable—we *were* both vulnerable; I was the lucky one; they got her, not me. Trouble was, they wouldn't let her go. They stayed with her."

"Meaning?"

"Meaning just that. They stayed with her; they stayed inside her somewhere. I don't know where. In her belly, in her intestines, in her heart. And they wouldn't let go of her. They made her get up and move around."

An image came to Ryerson then. It was an image from his childhood, when the same awful dream had tormented him for months. In the dream he entered a stone crypt. At the center of the crypt lay an open stone sarcophagus with a man inside dressed in a loose-fitting dirty white gown. When Ryerson drew closer, he could see that the man's face was yellow, his eyes large and round and pale, his lips a dull green. The man sat up. A kind of stiff, halting laugh came from him as if he were trying the laugh out to see if it still worked. He turned his head very mechanically, as if his neck were on dirt-encrusted ball bearings, and he said, "Boys! Bimbos! Beads!" in a high, hollow whisper that made his yellowish cheeks puff out briefly, then deflate. It should have been comical. It wasn't. Not from him. It was an image which had, then, pushed Ryerson screaming into wakefulness. Now it merely made him cringe.

"When?" he asked.

"When she was buried," Joan answered.

"Of course."

"So I had to stop her. For her own good, I had to stop her."

"Yes?"

"I got a shovel. I went to where she was buried. In the Edgewater Cemetery, near Erie. You've been there, haven't you?"

"Yes."

"I went there at night. When the moon

was new, so it was very dark. Lila walked when the moon was full." She paused. "I took my shovel to her grave and I began to dig." She stopped, looked questioningly at Creosote, then at Ryerson. "I'm sorry; it just occurred to me that I probably insulted your dog when I said he looked like the demons that I see."

"He'll survive," Ryerson said.

"Yes," Joan said. "And I dug Lila up." She looked momentarily astonished. "I dug her up; I dug my friend's body up! Rye, I dug and I dug and I dug! And then I shot her!"

The woman who called herself Loni was aware of a vague sensation of pressure where Laurie Drake had popped out from inside her, and if she had bothered to look, she would have seen that not only was the white blouse ripped from under her arm to where it tucked beneath the black skirt, but that a gaping creamy-pink gash rimmed by jagged protruding ribs and what passed for internal organs were visible beneath. But she didn't bother to look because she was involved in other things. Most important, she was involved in being alive, in being aware of herself and of the people on Baldridge Street, five blocks from Lawrence, only a couple of blocks from the area called "The District." The people were, predictably, looking slack-mouthed at her because they had never before seen such an incredible wound as hers.

"Hello," she cooed to a young man walking toward her; he was dressed in a neat but casual way, as if to take someone to a movie. "My name's Loni. What's yours?"

He hadn't seen her wound, yet; it was on her left side; he was approaching obliquely from her right. And though he had seen the half-dozen or so other people on Baldridge Street staring at her, he thought it was merely because she was so wonderfully attractive.

"My name's Benny," he said, a huge smile crinkling his pink, scrubbed face. How marvelous and how unbelievable, he thought, that this *woman* should be talking to him, that she should even be looking at him the way she was. Damn, it was like a dream. "Benny Bloom," he added; he had stopped walking and was letting her move closer to him. He still had not seen the wound at her left side, and because his attention was now solely on her, he did not see either that some of the slack-mouthed stares of the other people on the street had changed to stares of fear and revulsion, as if something unspeakably obscene had just been dropped into their midsts. One of these onlookers, a young woman wearing white jeans, said to Loni, "Miss, you're hurt; can I help you?" and though Benny heard the woman, her words did not register. He said again, "My name's Benny."

Loni stopped a few feet away; she was turned obliquely to him so her wound still was not visible. Benny added, "My real name is Benjamin."

"Miss," said the same young woman in white jeans, who now reached out to touch Loni's arm, "you're hurt; do you know you're hurt? Can I—"

Loni's movements were incredibly quick. She swung out with her left arm, hand wide, fingers arched, as if her hand were a claw, and caught the young woman in the ear, first, and tore it off, then, nails digging deep into the skin, ripped away half the woman's cheek before the woman fell to the sidewalk screaming in pain; she pushed herself to a kneeling position almost at once.

Benny Bloom could not believe what he was seeing. He smiled nervously. "Jumpin' criminy!" he whispered. Then, deep inside him, some slumbering sense of chivalry and heroism awoke and he threw his arms around Loni as if giving her a bear hug from behind. "No!" he screamed. "Stop it, stop it!" And as he screamed he was dimly aware of the incredible strength he felt in her. He squeezed harder.

"No!" Loni screamed.

"No!" Benny screamed.

And on the sidewalk, the young woman in white jeans moaned in pain and confusion.

Loni's upper body bent forward; Benny came with it, feet lifting from the sidewalk.

"Let her go!" he heard a man holler from close by.

Loni began to back toward the store window behind her.

"Let her go!" the same man said.

On the sidewalk the woman in white jeans had seen the blood pooling beneath her and she began to scream.

Loni screamed, too. So did Benny.

A cop appeared at the other side of the street just as the woman in white jeans fainted from shock and collapsed face forward to the sidewalk.

The cop, not understanding what he was seeing, drew his gun and pointed it at Benny Bloom. "Stop—" the cop began.

Loni backed Benny into the store window; his feet hit it and it shattered inward. Benny screamed again.

"Stop now!" the cop ordered.

Loni lurched forward, Benny still clinging to her, though now as much out of a paralytic fear as chivalry.

"Goddammit, I am ordering you to stop what you are doing now!" the cop screamed. He gave it a second. And another. Then he fired.

Benny Bloom felt a searing hot pain in his arm.

He fell.

Above him, Loni hesitated for only a fraction of a second. Then she bolted to her right. Within seconds she disappeared down an alleyway that led to the area called "The District."

The cop pointed frantically at the woman in white jeans, who was lying flat on her belly. He screamed, "Someone call for an ambulance," and went in pursuit of Loni.

Ryerson said, "Let me get you a drink."

Joan nodded, head lowered into her hands, elbows on the kitchen table. She'd been crying for several minutes. It was a cry of shame, and relief; shame for what she'd confessed, relief that she'd confessed it at last.

"Sure, anything," she murmured.

"Where do you keep it?" Ryerson asked.

She lifted her head from her hands, looked up at him, made a valiant, quivering attempt at a smile. "You don't know everything, do you, Rye?"

He shook his head. "Not everything," he said, and smiled back.

She nodded toward the living room. "There's a small cabinet in there, next to the couch. Get something for yourself, too."

"Thanks," he said, found the cabinet, got Joan a Scotch—because bottles of Dewar's Scotch outnumbered anything else, he figured Scotch was her drink—got himself a glass of ginger ale, and took the drinks back into the kitchen. He found Joan peering into the refrigerator. She looked up at him. "Hungry, Rye?"

He shrugged. "I could eat." He wasn't hungry, but he knew that eating was a way that some people, like Joan, put emotional outbursts behind them.

"Eggs okay?"

"Whatever you're having." He glanced about. "Where's Creosote?"

Joan glanced about, too. "I saw him here a few moments ago."

Creosote trotted in from the bathroom, down the hall from the kitchen, with a pink slipper in his mouth. Ryerson rushed over to him, scooped him up, and tore the slipper from his mouth. "No. Bad dog! Bad dog!"

Joan laughed; Ryerson looked at her, astonished, then at Creosote, then at the slipper which, he realized sinkingly, had been whole when Creosote had it in his mouth, but was now in two pieces, the top and the bottom, joined by a slender pink thread. He held the two pieces up in front of his nose, while Creosote sniffed desultorily at them, as if they had suddenly lost their interest. Ryerson said, "Gosh, I'm sorry, Joan; first your jacket, and now your slipper—"

Joan, still laughing—a laugh that had only the whisper of strain in it—said, "No, please, Rye; it's only a slipper. I never wore it, anyway. Let him have it."

Again Ryerson looked from her to Creosote

to the mangled slipper. "Are you sure?" he said.

Joan's laughter subsided. "Sure I'm sure."

Ryerson put the slipper to Creosote's muzzle; Creosote licked it disinterestedly, then squirmed to be let down. Ryerson said, shrugging, "I don't think he wants it, Joan."

She said quietly, simply, "I like you, Rye."

It caught him off guard. He said, Creosote still squirming to be let down, "Thanks. I like you, too."

"Good." She nodded at Creosote. "You can let him down. It's nice to have an animal around the house again." A pause. "And if you don't mind, Rye, I'd like to talk some more about Lila."

The woman who called herself Loni had left the luckless Alan Pierce's front door wide open, so his body and Laurie Drake were discovered only ten minutes later, four minutes after the shooting on Baldridge Street, by Alan's next-door neighbor, Mrs. Sibbe—a tall, gray-haired, officious-looking welfare worker—who phoned the police to report what she'd found, hesitated, put her hand to her stomach, went on. "Forty-two Lawrence Street, Apartment six B," then hung up, went into her bathroom, and vomited.

She was pretty much pulled together when the police arrived five minutes later. She watched as Detective Guy Mallory bent over the body of Alan Pierce, who was half lying, half sitting against the doorjamb, with his chin on his chest, eyes open, and his pupils rolled up in their sockets. Mallory put his finger to Pierce's left jugular, got no pulse there, then stepped aside for a man in white who had a Medivac emblem on his shoulder. "Looks like he's had it," Mallory said. Mrs. Sibbe then watched as Mallory bent over the naked Laurie Drake, who was still in the fetal position, her body covered with a creamy yellowish substance, like melted butter. Laurie's breathing was very shallow. It was the first time that Mrs. Sibbe had seen that Laurie's thumb was in her mouth, and she stepped forward from her apartment and announced, "I didn't know that girl was alive. If I'd known she was alive, I would have called for an ambulance, too."

Mallory glanced at her. "It's okay, ma'am; an ambulance was called just in case." He turned to Laurie Drake, then glanced at the man in white and said, "Give me some help with this one." The man in white nodded, came over, felt Laurie's pulse, turned to an ashen-faced uniformed cop who had just appeared, and said, "Get a blanket, would you?" The cop nodded dully and started into the apartment, apparently to find the bedroom. Mallory called, "No, no; Jesus, you'll mess up whatever evidence there is in there. Get a blanket from your car."

The cop, a rookie, answered unsteadily, "Oh. Sure. Sorry," and quickly disappeared down the stairway. He came back several minutes later, blanket in hand, and gave it to Mallory.

That's when Captain Lucas showed up. "There's been a shooting over on Baldridge Street, Guy."

Mallory looked up at him. "Oh?"

Lucas nodded. "Yeah. A cop shot a kid who was attacking some woman—at least that's what I got over the radio. The ambulance is on the way, but I'd like you to check it out and give this cop a hand. Spurling's there, but he's just about useless—"

Mallory, confused, interrupted, "But Jack, what about all this—"

Lucas stuck his hand out. "Give me your notebook. I'll take over."

Reluctantly, Mallory obeyed.

It was the smell that Lucas noticed first. It wasn't a bad smell; it wasn't gut-wrenching. It was almost pleasant—an acidic bitter sweetness, like concentrated lemon juice.

And it came to him—as he stood in the doorway to Alan Pierce's apartment and studied the awful scene in front of him—that he had encountered that smell before.

A uniformed cop appeared behind him. "Captain Lucas?"

"Yeah?" Lucas barked.

"I thought you should know; that boy, Benny Bloom, is going to be all right."

"What boy?"

"The boy who got shot on Baldridge Street."

"No one's named Benny Bloom."

"Sorry, Captain, but *he* is. Benjamin Bloom. They took him to Buffalo Memorial with a gunshot wound to the right arm."

"Uh-huh. And what about this woman who was attacked?"

"Which one, Captain?"

"What do you mean, which one? The one this *boy*, this Benny Bloom attacked, for Christ's sake!"

"Sorry. Two women were attacked, sir. One of the women"—he checked his notebook—"her name is Lilian Janus, was attacked by another woman; we don't have her name, yet. But this Janus woman is a mess, sir. Her face was torn to shreds. And the other woman ran off after the shooting."

"Ran off? To where?"

The cop shrugged. "Into The District, I think. We've got people looking for her right now."

"The district? What district?"

"Sorry, sir. That's what it's called. 'The District.' It's where all those abandoned buildings are—"

"Oh, yes," Lucas cut in. "Yes, I know what you're talking about. You said some people went after this woman. What people?"

Again the cop shrugged. "A couple of uniforms, Captain. The cop who shot this Benny Bloom is one of them, and Detective Spurling—"

"Yes," Lucas said, "I know about Spurling." He studied the grim scene in Alan Pierce's apartment for a moment, then said to the cop, "Thanks. That will be all. Keep me informed."

Gail Newman was at Buffalo Memorial, in a private room on the third floor. Benny Bloom was at Buffalo Memorial, too, in Intensive Care on the first floor. X-rays had shown that fragments of the bullet that struck his arm had ricocheted into his chest, lodging near his right ventricle, and the physician in charge in Intensive Care, Dr. Chandler, had decided to open him up. So, while Benny lay half awake in Intensive Care, awaiting surgery, Gail Newman was playing solitaire two floors above.

And five miles away, Ryerson Biergarten was seeing things.

"Rye?" Joan coaxed. "Is something wrong?"

They were in her living room. Ryerson was in an upholstered rocking chair with Creosote in his lap, the soft plastic duck held loosely in his mouth; Joan was in a wing chair nearby. They had begun to talk about Lila Curtis, but Joan had gotten no more than half a sentence out when Ryerson's eyes glazed over, his mouth opened slightly, and it became clear that his attention had suddenly changed focus.

"Rye?" Joan said again.

He stiffly turned his head toward her.

"Oh," he murmured, "I'm sorry. I guess I was somewhere else." It was clear, even as he spoke, that he still was somewhere else.

The soft plastic duck fell to the floor as Creosote nodded off. Ryerson glanced at the duck, leaned over as if to pick it up, straightened, glanced at Joan, then lifted his head a little so his gaze appeared to be on the living room wall.

"Talk to me, Rye?" Joan said.

"Yes," he whispered, and began idly stroking Creosote. "Yes," he whispered again.

In his mind's eye, he was seeing the soft, pretty pale blue of an early morning sky.

Joan asked, "Can I get you something?"

He said nothing. In his lap, Creosote began to gurgle raggedly.

Normally, the field of soft, pale blue that Ryerson was seeing would have been very pleasant. But there were dark gray smudges here and there on it, like pieces of a gathering storm. It had a kind of acid bittersweet smell, too, and Ryerson thought in so many words, *That's odd*.

Then the half-dozen smudges darkened on the field of pale blue so they were like holes in the daylight. And they began to move. Ryerson watched them for several moments, fascinated, until he realized that they were converging, that they were coming together. And, at last, he knew dimly what he was seeing.

He screamed.

The Devouring 161

Creosote woke in an instant, vaulted from his lap, and darted from the room.

And Joan, in the wing chair, stiffened up, with her eyes wide and her fists tightly clenched, as if Ryerson were about to attack her.

Part Three

Chapter Fourteen

In "The District"

Officer Leonard McGuire was breathing heavily from the adrenaline pumping through him. It had been a good five minutes anyway since he'd caught sight of any of the others searching for the woman who'd been attacked on Baldridge Street and he was getting very nervous.

He was on the edges of "The District." Visible only a block away was a street of trendy shops that were in stark contrast to this place. There were several smells here— the smell of urine combined with an acrid burning odor from the smelters two miles away, and the occasional stifling and stale odor of death from the vermin and stray cats that roamed the area. McGuire wondered if those odors ever found their way to that fashionable street. He decided that the shopowners had probably had a zoning ordinance passed against it.

He wasn't sure if he should draw his gun. Certainly he didn't need it to protect himself from the woman they were looking for—she was a victim, wasn't she? Of course, that fact posed two questions: If she was a *victim*, why had she run? And why to here? Good questions, he thought. And until he had the answers, it was wisest to play it safe. He unbuttoned the strap on his holster and withdrew his .38.

He had his back to the high windowless cement wall of an abandoned jeep factory. As he inched along the wall to the corner, and peered around it, deeper into "The District," he imagined that he smelled the tangy odor of oil mixed with other, far less pleasant smells.

He heard suddenly, from perhaps a hundred yards farther into "The District," "We only want to help you. Please come out." He didn't recognize the voice. "We only want to help you," the voice repeated urgently. "Please come out. Please tell us where you are."

And from deeper in "The District," he heard, "Detective Spurling. Over here!"

McGuire broke position and ran at a sturdy, fast clip toward the voice, his .38 pointed skyward.

Detective Third Grade Andrew Spurling thought, *Hell, this is more like it! No more damned bad check warrants; now I'm going to get a little action.* He was standing to one side of an open doorway, the cop who'd shot Benny Bloom was on the other. Spurling looked at the cop's name tag; he whispered, "What'd you hear, Mathilde?"

Officer Mathilde whispered back, "I heard someone groan in there." He nodded to indicate the darkened interior of the big red brick building; 40 years earlier, tank treads had been manufactured there.

"Male or female?" Spurling asked.

Mathilde smiled to himself. "It was kind of a neuter groan, Detective."

"Uh-huh," Spurling said. From behind him he heard the sound of running feet. He looked. McGuire was closing fast on them. Spurling waved urgently at him. McGuire veered off to the right. "Damned rookies," Spurling said to Officer Mathilde.

Mathilde smiled and nodded.

McGuire came up behind Spurling. "What's up?"

Spurling nodded urgently toward the doorway.

McGuire asked, "Is the perp in there?"

"Perp?" said Spurling.

Mathilde whispered from the other side of the doorway, gun drawn now, "He means 'perpetrator,' Detective."

"What perpetrator?" Spurling asked.

McGuire answered, "The one in there, the one inside."

"He means the woman," Mathilde whispered.

And the three of them heard another low groan from within the building.

Spurling called, "Are you all right?"

Another groan.

"You in the building; are you all right? Are you hurt?"

Silence.

Spurling sighed. "I'm going in there. Cover me."

Mathilde nodded. McGuire nodded.

And Spurling launched himself into the building. He tucked, rolled, came up on one knee, gun pointed into the darkness. He heard a shuffling noise just ahead, as if someone were moving toward him across the huge room. He strained to see, but the fading daylight filtering into the building showed him little; he'd have to wait for his eyes to adjust to the darkness, he realized. "Stay right where you are!" he bellowed. He saw a shift in the darkness, a quick dull flash of green. "Stay right there!" He glanced quickly back toward the doorway. "Mathilde, McGuire, come in here." He heard them move through the doorway.

"Jesus, it's dark in here," McGuire said.

"Flashlight," Mathilde said, and moments later McGuire shone the strong white beam of a flashlight into the darkness.

And caught the midsection of a tight green dress. He raised the flashlight. A woman's face—huge brown eyes, full red lips—appeared. These words, velvet and sensual and inviting, came from it: "Welcome, welcome. I have need of you."

The Following Day
Item from the *Buffalo Evening News*

Psychic says: "Watch out, Buffalo"

Nationally acclaimed psychic Ryerson H. Biergarten said yesterday that a "psychic storm" is brewing in Buffalo and that residents would do well to keep their doors and windows locked.

"I'm not sure of the focus of this storm," he explained. "I can say only that I have sensed extremely powerful forces at work in the underbelly of this city, and that these forces, if allowed to gain a foothold, could cause a great deal of trouble."

While he apologized for seeming to be an alarmist, Mr. Biergarten said it is the first time in his career as a psychic investigator that he has made such a pronouncement. "This psychic storm seems to be the result of the commingling of a number of psychic influences—all of them very, very real," he added.

Asked to characterize the source of this psychic storm, Biergarten apologized yet again and explained that the only word that came to him would, as he put it, "play havoc with my credibility, although I believe that in this instance it describes very real and very dangerous entities."

That word? "Demons," Biergarten said.

The Same Day
Item from the *Buffalo Daily News*

Bizarre Incident on Baldridge Street

Authorities are still investigating the police shooting of Benjamin Bloom, 16, on Baldridge Street yesterday afternoon. According to Tenth Precinct Captain Jack Lucas, Bloom was shot by Officer Isaac Mathilde while Bloom appeared to be in the process of attacking an unidentified woman. That woman is alleged to have attacked, in turn, 33-year-old Lilian Janus, of Buffalo. Mrs. Janus is listed in satisfactory condition with severe facial lacerations at Buffalo Memorial Hospital.

The woman allegedly attacked by Benjamin Bloom is still being sought at this time. She was last seen in the Arnsworth and Peacock Street section of the city, an area commonly known as "The District."

A connection between this incident and a murder on Lawrence Street has definitely been ruled out, according to Captain Lucas.

Captain Lucas leaned back in his desk chair and put his hands behind his head. "Enlighten me, Mr. Biergarten," he said, "just what sort of *demons* are you talking about?"

Ryerson, who was seated in front of Lucas's desk, answered, "I can tell you only what I saw, and how I interpreted it."

"You mean in this 'vision' of yours? I'll bet you have lots of visions, right, Mr. Biergarten?"

Ryerson sighed. "Can you forget your animosity for just a moment? I'm trying to tell you that your city is in trouble, for God's sake—"

"And do you know that I could have charges of incitement filed against you, Mr. Biergarten? What in the hell did you go to the newspapers for?"

Ryerson ignored the remark; he began, "Captain, there are indeed, as I told the reporter, *entities* in this city—"

Lucas came forward suddenly, slapped his hands hard on the top of the desk. " 'Visions,' 'entities'?!—for Christ's sake, man, you sound like you've got rats loose in your head!"

Ryerson asked pointedly, "Why did you let me in here to talk to you, Captain?"

The question took Lucas aback. He stared at Ryerson for a few moments, then he stammered, "Well, Jesus ... somebody's got to keep you in line."

Ryerson shook his head. "No. You let me in here because you know that what I'm saying is true, because you *know* that these ... these *entities* I'm talking about are real—"

Lucas pushed himself to his feet, his face beet red from anger. "I want you out of my city, Mr. Biergarten! I am *ordering* you to get out of my city!"

Ryerson calmly shook his head. "You don't have that right, Captain, and you know it." He stood, winced against the psychic onslaught of Lucas's anger, went on. "What have you got now? Four people dead? Five? By the time the week is done, that number will probably triple."

Lucas pointed stiffly at the door. "Get out!"

Ryerson nodded. "We'll talk again," he said. And even as he said it, he read again, as he had during their first meeting, something within the man that shamed him so much he hid it even from himself. And he read this, too: The man did not look ahead. His outlook on himself was very, very limited. Most people thought of themselves not only in terms of the past, but also in terms of the future—what *has* been, and what *will be*, so the picture that presented itself to Ryerson was usually very broad. Not so with Lucas. Ryerson could see only half of the picture. Only the past. And he wasn't at all sure why.

* * *

Benny Bloom's surgery had gone well and he was recovering in a semi-private room on the hospital's second floor, near the maternity wing. He'd already received a lot of get-well cards and they festooned the area around his bed. On a small roll-about table there was a cute card from his playful Aunt Greta ("Hospitals," it read, "are okay if you don't mind," flip the page, "surly nurses, doctors with bad breath, cardboard food, basic beige, a morgue in the basement, going broke to get well—and that reminds me— get well soon!") and near it a handmade card from his Uncle Floyd, who wrote miserably confessional poetry for various small literary magazines, and around those two, arranged in a neat semi-circle—Benny had a wide streak of orderliness—there were half a dozen cards from classmates at Buffalo Pierpont High School, where he was a senior much liked by the high honor roll crowd.

On the floor, again set up in a semi-circle, were six more cards. One was from his mom, who'd written on the envelope, "To my little boy—may he feel no pain," another was from a great-aunt who saw herself as something of a homey, if confusing, philosopher; her card went on and on, in her own hand, about the rightness of suffering and pain, "if only," it proclaimed, "as a state of looking backwardness and gaiety yet to come." Benny took pleasure and consolation from all these cards. They told him that there were lots of people in the world who cared about him, regardless of the fact that he was more than a little odd.

He said now, to a young nurse named Carlotta Scotti, a tall, olive-skinned brunette who had only recently earned her R.N., "You're not surly at all, Carlotta."

She looked bemusedly at him. "Thank you, I guess," she said.

He nodded at his Aunt Greta's card. "That card says nurses are surly. But I think you're great." His voice was strong and sure, although the rest of him was still weak from surgery.

"I think you're great, too, Benny." She put one hand below his right shoulder, the other on his right thigh. "Do you think you could turn over just a little bit?" she said, and, with his help, she turned him so his buttock was exposed. "Hold it there for just a moment, Benny."

His head was turned away. She heard a strange, soft giggle come from him.

"We're not going to be using the needle today, Benny."

"I don't mind needles," he said.

"Well *I* do," said Nurse Scotti, smiling at his machismo.

"I really do think you're great," Benny said.

"Quiet now," said Nurse Scotti.

Another strange, soft giggle came from Benny, a little stranger than the first, a little less soft. "That didn't hurt at all, Carlotta," he said.

"I haven't done it yet," she said.

"Do it then," he said.

Chapter Fifteen

Detective Guy Mallory threw back his head and downed a small glass of Genny Cream Ale: he followed it immediately with a shot of whiskey. Then he leaned over the bar and nodded grimly. "Yes," he said to Detective Spurling, "I'd have to agree, Andy; that was just about the nastiest thing I've ever seen."

Spurling harrumphed. "You think what you had to deal with was nasty! Jesus Christ, that thing *we* found—"

"It's amazing Lucas could keep it out of the papers."

Spurling shrugged. "Why not. Just a wino; nobody cares about winos." He downed the rest of his beer. "Probably a half-dozen dead winos in there."

"I wouldn't be surprised," Mallory said. He grinned. "Well, at least you guys found something."

"Oh, gimme a break," Spurling growled. "What do you think I am—an amateur? I knew what I was doing in there, and like I told the captain—shit, there was nothing to find. Except that damned wino. And a thousand rats."

Mallory's grin froze on his face. "What are you getting so hot about?"

Spurling nervously sipped his glass of Michelob. He grimaced. "This stuff doesn't taste the same as it used to," he muttered. He glanced at Mallory. "Sorry. I guess I've been a little on edge lately."

"Yeah," Mallory said, "tell me about it."

Spurling shrugged. "I haven't been sleeping, you know? And I ain't had no appetite, either. Nerves, I guess." He took another sip of the Michelob, grimaced again. "Everything *tastes* like the *stuff* that wino was covered with smelled. Maybe that's why I ain't been eating." He pushed the glass away from him on the bar. "How's your partner doing? She on the mend?"

"She'll survive," Mallory answered, "she's tough—maybe even as tough as she thinks she is." He smiled, pleased by his observation. "That damned kid sucked her blood? Did you know that?"

Spurling nodded. "Yeah, I knew it. Jesus." He put his hand to his stomach.

Mallory said, "Hey, you okay?"

"Sure." Spurling closed his eyes tightly, in pain. "It's this damn beer, I think—I don't know." He took his hand from his stomach, sighed in relief. "It comes and goes, Guy," he explained. "Maybe I got an ulcer or something."

And Mallory said, "I think you've got wormy winos on the brain, Spurling."

The uniformed cop who shot Benny Bloom was a twenty-two-year veteran of the force named Isaac Mathilde. The name, which suggested gentleness, sophistication, and learning, did not suit him on the job, when he climbed into his tough-as-nails, don't-mess-with-me character. But when he left work, and went home to his books, his flowers, and his cats, it fit him beautifully. He even looked the part: he was thin, dark-haired, dark-eyed, smooth-faced, graceful-looking. That side of him—his gentleness, sophistication, and learning—was in agony. He'd requested and had been granted a week's leave of absence because of that agony and now, at 10:30 P.M., five days after the shooting, he was sitting in his shade-darkened living room with a small glass of Grand Marnier in hand and Debussy's *Prelude to the Afternoon of a Faun* on the stereo. It suited his mood of guilt and self-doubt. It fed it.

In his twenty-two years on the force, he had never before even drawn his gun, let alone fired it. And now he had come damned close to killing some kid with the unlikely name of Benny Bloom, who, it turned out, was only trying to be a Good Samaritan.

And who in God's name had given him, Isaac Mathilde, the kind of power that had allowed him to step in and make a snap decision that had nearly ended Benny Bloom's life? Who had given him that power, who had authorized it, what moral right did he have? Who had let loose the foul creature who'd been strutting about for twenty-two years as if the world were answerable to his whim and his weapon?

And why, in the past three days, had he found that creature so terribly strong within him?

One of Isaac's cats came into the darkened room. The cat was a small and sleek Siamese whose favorite spot was on the wide mantel over the fireplace, five feet up from the floor. The cat eyed the mantel, settled back on its haunches, and leaped.

"Good Samson," Isaac said, as the cat lay down on the mantel and began cleaning itself with slow and graceful deliberation.

Isaac took another sip of the Grand Marnier, then poured some more from the bottle on the delicate cherry table near his chair. He'd never gotten drunk on Grand Marnier before and he wondered if it was even possible to get drunk on it.

But hell, what did it matter now?

On the mantel, Samson began to purr loudly. Isaac lifted his glass to him: "To all the sleek and sophisticated cowards in this world, Samson. To you and me!" And he downed the Grand Marnier in one swallow.

Then he lifted his .38 from the table near his chair, put the barrel into his mouth, and pulled the trigger.

At that very moment Lilian Janus was saying to her reflection in her bathroom mirror, "Well, you were never *that* beautiful anyway." Then she immediately turned away from the mirror and began to weep.

From the bedroom adjoining the bathroom her husband Frank called, "Lily? Are you all right?"

She nodded, face in her hands, left hand covering the bandages that swathed that side of her face. The doctors at Buffalo Memorial had made a heroic effort to sew the skin and the ear back, but had warned her that the probability was she'd lose the ear, and that since the skin over her cheek had suffered too much trauma, she'd probably have to have skin grafted from her thigh, instead.

Lilian Janus was a passive, unassuming, gentle person. At thirty-three, she was the mother of twin seven-year-old boys, and a ten-year-old girl. She belonged to the PTA, the Buffalo Arts and Crafter's Club, the Young Republican Women's Club, and she regularly submitted "Life in These United States" anecdotes to the *Reader's Digest*, hoping to make a quick $500. At least twice a month she wrote letters to the editors of various newspapers in the area. She wrote about zoning laws, leash laws, massage parlors, and Bingo games, which she described as "ill-disguised gambling schemes." She had a part-time job as a cosmetics salesperson at Sibley's Department Store.

Her husband appeared in the bathroom doorway. He was a muscular, hairy, handsome man with a cleft in his chin and a twinkle in his eye. He was dressed only in a towel, which he held at his waist. "C'mon, babe," he said, "it's not as bad as you think. So you lose an ear?" He was, of course, trying to be flippant, and therefore comforting. "You can still hear out of it; that's what the doctors said."

Lilian let her hands drop slowly. She blubbered, "Whether I ca-can *hear* out of it doesn't make *any* di-difference, Frank. It *looks* ugly!"

"So you cover it with your hair. You've got nice hair, Lily." He let his towel drop.

Her mouth fell open. "What are you doing?" she whispered.

He shrugged. "Hell, I thought we could make love. It *is* Thursday, you know."

"No, it isn't. It's Friday."

Again he shrugged. "So? Who says that just because it's Friday we can't make love? You want to know the truth, Lily?"

"The truth?" She put her hand to her stomach.

He nodded vigorously. "The truth. And the truth is, I like you ... uh, like that."

"Like what?"

"Like that. In bandages."

"You like me ..." She winced against the sudden pain in her belly.

"In bandages," Frank repeated. "I like you in bandages."

"I don't understand," Lily said. "I don't think I *want* to understand." She glanced at his penis. "Please, Frank, cover that up, would you?"

"You never asked me to cover it up before."

"Well, it was never so . . . so *obvious* before."

"That's because you were never so appealing before, Lily."

With her left hand she again covered her stomach, where the pain had redoubled. And with her right hand she reached out and slammed the bathroom door shut. She did it so quickly, and took Frank so by surprise, in fact, that the door slammed hard into his erection and he screamed in pain.

Seconds later, his voice trembling with anger, and with pain, he pounded on the door. "Open up now, Lily! You open up now, or this door's coming down. And that's not a threat! That's a promise!"

"Frank, please," she pleaded. "I don't feel well. Please go away. I'm sorry I hurt you." And even as she said the words, she realized that she'd been right all along, that what she'd suspected these past twelve years of her marriage to Frank Janus had been true. He was a lecherous, unseemly, brutish dolt, and she deserved far, far better.

For Ryerson Biergarten, the act of making love was an unpredictable experience, as it is for everyone. There were good times and bad times, and the bad times were always better than no lovemaking at all. And there were times when it looked like bad or just so-so lovemaking was going to happen and it turned out to be great, and there were times when what looked like great turned out just so-so. Such things could never be counted on.

What made the experience great for Ryerson was how much *intermingling* there was—not just the intermingling of bodies, pleasant as that could be, but the intermingling of souls and psyches, too. When for a precious few seconds, the lovers intermingled them*selves*, their lives, and sum totals. When they opened themselves up and swallowed each other.

He thought that that was what had happened with Joan Mott Evans, who lay beside him on her bed. She had been lying quietly beside him for a good ten minutes, while her breathing slowed and softened. They were naked on top of a blue quilt; a night-light burned at the other side of the room.

Ryerson, the first to speak, said, "That was beautiful, Joan."

She said nothing. He could sense a feeling of comfort and contentment from her. For another minute or so he stayed quiet, then he added, "You're beautiful."

She covered her hand with his. She whispered, "I think this is the start of something, Rye."

In the semi-darkness, he said, "I'm smiling."

"And?" she said.

"And what?"

"And anything else, Rye?"

He nodded. "Oh. Yes." He turned over on his side. She turned, faced him. He lovingly stroked her cheek, her neck, the slope of her breast.

At the other side of the closed bedroom door, Creosote began to whimper. Ryerson said to Joan, "He and I have grown very attached."

"Uh-huh," she said. "Well, let's you and me grow attached, okay."

"I'd like that very much," he whispered.

In Room 1512 of the Buffalo Memorial Hospital, Laurie Drake was still in the fetal position, still had her thumb in her mouth and her eyes open; nearby, a device had been set up to drip a mild salt solution into her eyes every few seconds, so they wouldn't dry out.

"We're getting some response," said Dr. Wayne Chandler to Guy Mallory.

"Oh?" Guy said, uncertain what the doctor

was referring to and unwilling to let him know it.

Chandler nodded. "Her EKGs have altered since she was brought in, and now and then she appears to look around the room—moving her eyes only, of course."

"Of course," Mallory said.

"Her coma is deep," Chandler went on, "though not so deep that we see no hope for recovery. I do think she'll be with us a good long time. A month, perhaps. Maybe longer."

Mallory sighed. "Jesus, Doc—"

"Doctor," Chandler corrected him, then smiled an apology. "I'm sorry—I just have this aversion to 'Doc.' You understand, I'm sure."

Mallory said, "Yeah, I understand. I was going to say that I've seen a few like her. You know—people in comas, and I have to ask myself what the hell is going on in their heads. Where they are, you know. Because if they're not here, with us, where *are* they?"

Chandler nodded. "It's a question all of us ask, Detective. And I wish I could answer it."

But even Laurie Drake could not have answered that question, because language was beyond her, just as language is beyond any fetus. Which is what she was, essentially. A developing organism, something newly created, not yet whole—regardless of the physical evidence to the contrary. Inside her skull, her brain was struggling to renew itself, but in the process of conception, all that was Laurie Drake had been swept away, and a new Laurie Drake was emerging. Whether she would be as precocious as the old Laurie Drake, whether she would have a predilection for hot fudge sundaes, or would develop an early interest in the opposite sex, or be drawn to horror movies, all as the old Laurie Drake had been, was yet to be seen.

But that evening, while Ryerson Biergarten again made sweet and soul-consuming love to Joan Mott Evans, and Captain Jack Lucas lovingly cleaned his Colt .45, and Gail Newman slept a fitful sleep, and Detective Andy Spurling went on his shift—despite the awful pains in his stomach—and Lilian Janus kept herself locked in her bathroom, and Benny Bloom dreamed of Nurse Scotti, she—the new Laurie Drake—was destined to be one of the lucky ones.

Chapter Sixteen

The Following Morning

Irene Sabitch, in the Records Division of the Buffalo Police Department, asked her co-worker Glenn Coffman, "What do you know about Jack Lucas? He's the captain over at the Tenth Precinct."

Coffman glanced briefly at her from his own monitor. "Not a whole lot. I hear he's an asshole, that's about it." He looked at his monitor again.

"Well, if he is, he's got good reason for it."

Coffman glanced at her again. "Oh? Why's that?"

She answered simply, "He's dying."

Coffman shrugged. "That's tough. What of?"

"Cancer."

"How do you know?"

She nodded at her monitor. "It's part of the employee records, so I have access to it."

"*Limited* access, Irene. Those records are confidential—"

"I know that. I wasn't snooping. Too much, anyway. I was only trying to open that damned set of files, and his name came up, so—"

"How'd *his* name come up?"

"It was in the news articles about that murder/suicide in Erie. You remember, Lila Curtis—"

"So that's her name. Lila." He grinned. "I was pretty close. I said Lily, didn't I?"

"Yes, you did, congratulations. Anyway, Lucas was down there, in Erie, at the time. Apparently the Erie police chief is a close friend of his and since he was there, anyway, he asked him to help."

Coffman eyed her silently for several seconds. Then he said, "And you think that screwy user number is his—Lucas's?"

"I'm almost positive of it."

Coffman sighed. "Well, for God's sake, Irene, you've got a list of user numbers there; why don't you just find his—"

"I *did* that, and it didn't work."

"Well then, what you do is, you call up this Captain Lucas and you tell him, 'Captain Lucas, I have a disk here that I believe has your user number on it, but the user number on file doesn't work. Was it changed? Did you change it?'"

She nodded. "I did that, too. He says he

doesn't know a damn thing about it—and those were his words exactly. He even ordered me to stop looking into the whole thing."

"Why in hell would he do that if he doesn't know anything about it? It doesn't make sense."

"You're very good at stating the obvious, Glen."

"Uh-huh. So what did you tell him?"

"I told him okay, I'd close down the file, I'd erase it."

"And he believed you?"

"I don't think so. When I got to work this morning, the disk was missing."

"My God—"

She smiled, pleased with herself. "Good thing I took the precaution of making a copy."

At the Tenth Precinct

"Well, where is he then?" Ryerson asked the desk sergeant.

"Listen," the sergeant answered, "all I know is that Captain Lucas left the building at nine-thirty this morning. He didn't tell me where he was going and I didn't ask."

Ryerson shifted Creosote from one arm to the other; Creosote had his soft plastic duck between his teeth and as Ryerson shifted him, the dog growled as if annoyed.

"That's some dog," the desk sergeant quipped.

Ryerson ignored the remark. "Could you tell Captain Lucas that I was here?"

"And you are?"

"My name's Ryerson Biergarten."

The desk sergeant wrote it on a memo pad. "You're that psychic, right?"

Again Ryerson ignored him. "Is there a place called Frank's in Buffalo?"

"Frank's?" said the desk sergeant, turned, and called to a couple of uniformed cops behind him, "Hey, any you guys heard of a place called Frank's?"

One of the cops answered, "You mean Frank's Place? Yeah. It's on Eddy Street."

The desk sergeant turned back to Ryerson. "You got that?"

"I got it," Ryerson said.

"You know where Eddy Street is?"

"No," Ryerson answered, "but I have a map."

The sergeant grinned. "I thought you were psychic." A brief pause. "The hell with the map. What you do is, you go back out to the street, you turn left, you go five blocks, you make another left—" He paused, glanced back at the uniformed cops. "Hey, is Eddy Street north or south of Minerva?"

The same cop answered, "Minerva? Where's that?"

And Ryerson said, "Thanks, anyway. I'll stick with the map."

"Suit yourself," the desk sergeant said. And as Ryerson turned to go, he called, "You ain't gonna like it down there, believe me."

The image of a blue sky littered with dark gray smudges was with Ryerson almost constantly now, though he tried hard to put it aside. The blue was still soft, pale, and pretty, but the smudges moved and pulsated as if they were alive. There were perhaps half a dozen of them, Ryerson thought. He wasn't sure of the number because each time he tried to study them—much as he'd study a painting or a photograph—they shifted crazily, like snakes squirming off, and he found that his view of them was always oblique.

His guess was that each of the dark gray smudges represented, as he'd told Captain Lucas the day before, "an entity."

"An entity?" Lucas had said then, his voice dripping with incredulity. "What sort of *entity*, Mr. Biergarten?"

And despite himself, despite all that he knew about how to approach people like Jack Lucas—people who, as Lucas had put it, believed that "everything's got a logical explanation . . . if you can't touch it or smell it or taste it or fuck it, then by God it doesn't exist!"—Ryerson had answered, "An evil entity." Which elicited a half minute's worth of hooting laughter from Lucas—laughter so loud and uncontrolled, in fact, that one of the detectives in the outer office had stuck his head in and said, "Is everything okay here?"

But *evil entity* fit, Ryerson thought now, as he maneuvered the Woody down Minerva Street on his way to Eddy Street, then to Frank's Place, where, he was sure, he'd find Captain Lucas.

But there was this, too; if each of those obscenely pulsating dark gray smudges on a field of soft, pretty pale blue represented an evil entity—or, as Joan preferred it, a *demon*—then each of those smudges had to signify a person, too. Ryerson knew this as certainly as he knew that the sun would set, though it had taken Joan to make him see it clearly. "I don't know where they come from," she'd told him. "I guess they come from the same place that all suffering and loneliness and pain comes from. From us. From all of us."

He stopped for a red light at the corner of Minerva and Eddy streets. He looked first right, then left, hoping to see a sign that said "Frank's Place," but he saw only a succession of tattered two- and three-story brick buildings in both directions. Near the center of the block to his left there was a sign that read GREYHOUND PACKAGE EXPRESS, and beyond it a neon sign was flashing the word "EAT" in green. On impulse, he turned right.

Upon reflection now, he thought that Jack Lucas had had good reason to toss him out of his office, because he'd handled the whole thing badly. He'd let the grotesque and deadly scenario developing in Buffalo overcome his good sense. Because while "evil entity" had elicited a half minute's worth of hooting laughter from Captain Lucas, "demons" had gotten a full minute's worth of stony silence. Angry and unreadable silence. "I don't be*lieve* in demons!" he had said finally. "And I think that anyone who does is a child."

"Yes," Ryerson nodded, "I agree—that is, of course, if we're talking about the archetypal demon that climbs out of hell to take possession of us. And I'm not talking about that at all, Captain. I'm talking about the demons *we* create." That, Ryerson remembered, had clearly touched a raw nerve with Lucas.

"Whatever . . . problems any of us have, Mr. Biergarten," he'd begun, "are ours to deal with in our own way."

"You don't understand; I'm sorry, Captain, you don't understand. I'm not talking about psychic demons; I'm not talking about *behavior*, I'm talking about things we can touch, and feel, and taste—they're your criteria, after all. I'm talking, for instance, about this woman—"

And that's when Lucas had thrown him out.

Ryerson saw a small, weathered, handmade sign just ahead—dark blue letters on a white background: FRANK'S PLACE it read. He pulled over to the curb, locked all the Woody's doors, glanced about. There were a couple of haggard-looking men on the sidewalk, and, as Ryerson watched, they went into Frank's Place. Moments later he followed.

Benny Bloom knew that most of the kids at Buffalo Pierpont High School thought he was a nerd. But that was okay, because a nerd, by definition, was different, and different was usually better. It was all a matter of perception. Being *thought of* as a nerd was one thing, but actually *being* a nerd was something else entirely. *Being* a nerd was a privilege and an honor. If you were a nerd, it meant that you were above average, it meant that you were superior.

Or so Benny told himself.

In practice, Benny thought, being a nerd was a damned lonely business. The only people who wanted to hang around nerds were other nerds, and nerds as a group were boring.

Nerds didn't get any girls, either. Unless they were girl nerds.

And Benny Bloom wanted girls. Not girl nerds. He wanted the cheerleader types, the foxes with creamy white thighs and huge breasts and softly sculpted necks. The trouble was, the only ones who got those girls were jocks—the guys with meat for brains and tree limbs for arms, and pants three sizes too small at the crotch. The guys who could say "Hi, baby" and get away with it (Benny had said "Hi, baby" once, just to try it out, because he'd heard the jocks say it. "Baby?" asked the particular cheerleader type he was talking to. "What do you mean?" Benny shrugged. "Jeez, I don't know," he answered. "Just that, I guess. 'Hi, baby.' I was just trying to be friendly. I didn't mean anything by it. I'm sorry." "Don't mention it," said the girl, smiling to herself, and walked off).

And Benny had wondered more than once what it would be like to be a brainy jock, the kind of guy who could say "Hi, baby," and quote T. S. Eliot in the same breath.

"Hi, baby," he said now (at approximately the same time that Ryerson Biergarten, Creosote in his arms, was sitting down at the bar at Frank's Place), and Nurse Carlotta Scotti answered, "Sorry, Benny, but did you just say something?"

And turned away from her, his buttock exposed for yet another shot, he said again, "Hi, baby," and added in the same breath, "In the room the women come and go/ Talking of Michelangelo."

"What woman is that, Benny?" Nurse Scotti asked.

"Hi, baby," he said again.

And she said, half scoldingly, "No, Benny, please don't flex your buttock, it only makes it harder to get the needle in."

But Benny wasn't flexing his buttock. Benny was changing.

The bar at Frank's Place had a high sheen from too much varnish and was streaked with beer. When the bartender asked, "What's your poison?" he looked like he really meant it.

"Ginger ale," Ryerson answered.

"Uh-huh," said the bartender, raising a very thick and bushy eyebrow. "One tall ginger ale coming up."

"Actually," Ryerson said, as Creosote strained mightily to lick his chin, "I was looking for someone." He glanced about. Frank's Place was all but empty. At the rear the two haggard men who'd come in before him were seated at a small wooden table playing cards. At the opposite end of the bar a buxom woman in a tight green dress sipped at what looked like a water glass full of whiskey. As he glanced at her, she glanced at him, grinned, looked away. Ryerson repeated, "I was looking for someone, but I—"

"Her name's Doreen," said the bartender, and nodded at the woman in the green dress.

Ryerson said, "No, you don't understand. I was looking for a man."

"Not here you don't look for no man," the bartender growled.

"I'm afraid you still don't understand," Ryerson said. He stopped. An image had shot from the bartender's mind to his. "Have you got a back room?"

"A back room? What for?"

Ryerson shrugged. "For whatever."

"Yeah?" said the bartender, leaning over the bar. "What *kind* of whatever?"

Creosote finally found Ryerson's chin and gave it a long, loving lick.

The bartender nodded. "You talkin' about something with that dog? Is that what you're talking about, mister? If it is—"

Ryerson decided it was time to change the subject. "Do you know a man named Lucas?"

The bartender shook his head immediately. "Don't know no one named Lucas."

And from the opposite end of the bar the woman drawled, "Ah do."

Ryerson looked at her. She had the water glass full of whiskey poised at her lips. "Whatchoo want with old Lucas?" She took a slug of the whiskey, put it down hard. "You a friend a his? You don't look like no friend a his."

Ryerson got up from the barstool, went over to the woman, sat beside her.

Creosote began to whimper.

"Somethin' wrong which your dog?" the woman asked.

Creosote tried to burrow in between Ryerson's side and arm; Ryerson stroked him reassuringly. "Hey, it's okay, fella," he said, then, to the woman, "He comes here, doesn't he?"

"Lucas? Sure. He comes here. He's a friend a mine."

Ryerson found that he could read from her only what he usually read from crazies, and animals—what looked in his mind's eye like the snow between channels on a TV set. "A friend of yours?" he said, and wondered why she'd been so quick with information. "Is he here now? It's imperative that I get in touch with him."

"Imperative, is it?" said the woman. "Im*perative*?!" She grinned, took another sip of the whiskey, glanced down the front of her low-cut dress, reached in, and adjusted her bra.

Creosote's whimpering grew louder.

She went on. "Why don't you tell Doreen what's so im*perative*, and I'll *re*lay the message to him when he comes in."

The bartender brought Ryerson's glass of ginger ale; "Buck fifty," he said, and Ryerson dug in his pockets, found a dollar bill and some change, and put it on the counter.

Detective Third Grade Andy Spurling's fondest memories were of growing up in Syracuse, New York, where he was thought of as the toughest kid on the block, and the quickest with a six-gun. His six-guns, of course, were made by Mattel, but they were made of real metal, not plastic like they are today, and they were heavy, and their action was much like the action of a real gun. The one he carried now, for instance.

He was the toughest kid on the block because he was the biggest, and the most aggressive, and pain had never bothered him a lot—a fact which had put the other kids, even the smart ones, in awe of him (he remembered particularly the time he held the lit end of a cigarette against the back of his wrist; he remembered the acrid smell of burning flesh, the gasps of the kids gathered around him, his own tight sneer against the pain).

He knocked on the door of Apartment 3C at the Livemore Apartments—he had a bad-check arrest warrant in his suit coat pocket. He listened to the movement inside the apartment, tried to gauge just what kind of movement it was, whether someone was going out a window, or merely getting up from a chair. Funny, he thought, that the memories from his childhood should return with such vibrancy in the last few days, ever since that incredible mess on Lawrence Street.

"Yes, who is it?" he heard a man call from within the apartment.

"Police," he called back. And there was silence.

Maybe, he thought, the memories had returned because he'd realized at last that his position with the Buffalo Police Department was always going to be pretty low, that he was probably never going to make captain, or even lieutenant. Maybe he'd make sergeant if he tried really hard. Sure, twenty years before, in Syracuse, when he was a tough eleven-year-old kid who could hold lit cigarettes against the back of his wrist, he was top of the heap. But when you were grown-up, people had words other than "tough" to describe that sort of thing. They called it "stupid," and "juvenile," and even the assholes who hung out at sleazy bars weren't impressed by it anymore. What did impress lots of people, though, was gunplay. Eleven-year-olds, twenty-year-olds, thirty-year-olds—it didn't matter. Guns demanded respect. And Christ, but he was good with a gun!

"What do you want?" he heard from within Apartment 3C.

He put one hand on his .45, in a shoulder holster, and the other on his stomach, because, for the past five days, it had been giving him lots of trouble. "Mr. Warren Anderson?" he called.

"Who's asking?" the man called back.

"Are you . . ." A surge of pain; he winced. "Are you Warren Anderson?"

"No. He ain't here."

"Open the door, please."

"I said Warren ain't here. He went south. He went to Florida."

Spurling hesitated, hand tightening on the .45. What would Guy Mallory do now, he wondered, and another surge of pain pushed through him; he winced again, a small "Uh!" escaped him. How would that tough eleven-year-old kid from Syracuse react—not only to the pain, but to this man he had to haul in? The hell with Guy Mallory. Mallory was too cautious; Mallory followed the book, the damned criminal-coddling *book*.

"Listen," he called to the man in the apartment, "I've got an arrest warrant for Warren Anderson—"

"He ain't here. I *told* you that!"

"The amount of the check"—another surge of pain went through him, deeper; he doubled over, waited for it to subside. "The amount of the check is just twenty dollars. You pay it, Mr. Anderson, and you're free."

Silence.

"Mr. Anderson?" Spurling coaxed, and realized, with relief, that the pain in his stomach seemed to be subsiding.

"Twenty dollars?" the man called.

"That's all. Shit, if you haven't got it, I'll *loan* it to you."

"Yeah?"

"Sure." Spurling glanced at the floor; he had seen movement there. His gaze settled on his pants cuffs, which appeared to be hanging over his shoes much more than they usually did. He looked back at the door. "Sure," he called, again. "As long as you promise to pay me back, Mr. Anderson."

"Twenty dollars? That's all it is? Just twenty dollars?"

"That's all, Mr. Anderson. I've got it in my hands right now." Once more he glanced in confusion at his pants cuffs, then at the door again. Strange, he thought, but the apartment number seemed to be higher on the door than it had been five minutes before. "Why don't you do us both a favor, Mr. Anderson, and open up."

And inside the apartment, Warren Anderson wondered if the cop would indeed loan him the twenty dollars to cover the bad check. He opened the door.

And looked down at the kid standing there who was awash in clothes five sizes too large for his eleven-year-old frame.

Anderson muttered, "What in the hell—" and smiled a big smile of deep relief. His smile broadened when the kid produced a gun from inside his suit jacket and pointed it directly at Anderson's forehead. Anderson threw his hands into the air. "Hey, don't shoot me, kid!" he laughed. The kid fired. A .45-caliber bullet tore at a hard angle through Anderson's forehead, into his brain, out the other side, and imbedded itself high on the north wall of Apartment 3C.

At Frank's Place the woman named Doreen was getting off her barstool. "Nice talkin' to ya," she said, took one last tug on her glass of whiskey, called, "Hey, I'll see ya, Sam," to the bartender, who looked over and said, "Yeah, sure."

The Devouring

Then Ryerson asked her, "Who are you?"

"Name's Doreen," the woman answered.

"No, it isn't," Ryerson said, because for just one moment, one half second, the snow he was reading from her had lifted and he had caught a glimpse of something hard and dark and obscene beneath.

The woman smiled coyly. "Whatever I want to call myself, my man, then that's my name. I want to call myself Ginger Rogers, then that's what you gotta call me." She turned her back to him, glanced around. "Nice little dog you got there. Better watch out no one *steps* on him," and she laughed quickly, and left the bar.

The bartender watched her go, then turned to Ryerson. "That's one nasty dame," he said.

"Yes," Ryerson said, "she is that."

Chapter Seventeen

Lilian Janus, dressed in a pink vest and skirt, white blouse, nylons, and white Naturalizers for her part-time job at Sibley's Department Store, had been sitting for two hours on the edge of her bed with her eyes on the naked corpse of her husband. It lay on the floor on its stomach, arms out straight, legs together, feet pointing in opposite directions, head supported by the handsome, cleft chin.

She was noticing for the very first time that the hair on his legs ended abruptly at the tops of his thighs. Practically every other part of his body, even his shoulders and his back, was covered with curly black hair. She remembered how proud he was of that hair; she remembered that he said he looked "manful" with so much hair on his body.

She had already sent her children off to school. They'd asked, "Where's Daddy?" because he was almost never absent from the breakfast table, newspaper in one hand, coffee cup in the other. "He went to work early," she'd explained, which they had readily accepted.

She now had a pair of scissors in her hand. They were a good, sharp pair of hair-cutting scissors that she'd used countless times on her husband's and kids' heads, and she was transferring them from one hand to the other, blade to palm, handle to palm. As she did this, she was remembering the way her husband had tried to seduce her the night before, his erection bobbing up and down as if to beckon her to the bed with it.

"Damned pig!" she hissed at him. "Whoever killed you, I *thank* them!"

She'd developed a few theories about the murder. Perhaps, while she and Frank were asleep, a burglar had come into the house and had put a knife straight into his heart, just to be safe. Or perhaps Frank had gotten up to fix himself a ham sandwich and as he carried the knife about, he fell on it. That would account for the fact that the point of the knife was now protruding from his back just to the right of his spine.

She got off the bed, kneeled next to Frank's body, and settled back on her heels. She had the hair-cutting scissors clutched tightly in her right hand. She transferred them to her left, leaned forward, and whispered to Frank's corpse, "Even in death you're very manful, aren't you, Frank?"

She had another theory about his murder. It was, she thought, the least likely of all because it involved another woman. His lover.

She'd seen her, briefly, in the mirror over the bathroom sink—a woman with flashing green eyes, an exquisite oval face, and an air of murder and hate that hung about her like a shroud. Lilian had known about that woman for a long time. She'd often seen her in mirrors, though never as clearly as she had last night. She knew that the woman's name also was Lilian, which was not, she thought, a very strange coincidence, because Lilian was a common enough name.

That woman could have killed her husband, she decided.

The woman named Lilian who seemed to exist only in mirrors.

Last night she could have come out of the mirror and shoved a steak knife deep into Frank's heart and then laid his body out straight.

So she, the real Lilian, could cut that awful black hair from him.

She leaned over Frank's back. With the hand that held the scissors she put the tip of her finger to the tip of the knife and pressed on it till a trickle of blood started. She smiled, withdrew the finger, and began to snip.

* * *

Ryerson Biergarten said to Joan Mott Evans, "I can't shake it, Joan. It just sits there and I can't shake it."

Joan, seated next to him on the couch, their hands clasped, had a good idea what he was talking about, not only because he'd described it to her—the field of pale blue, the dark gray smudges—but because she could see it, too, after a fashion. Not as clearly as he saw it, it was true. And it didn't stick with her, either; it came and went randomly on waves of psychic interference. But she could sense what he sensed in it—the evil, the threat, the obscenity.

"They're people," Ryerson whispered.

"Yes," Joan said.

"People like Lila." He felt Joan's hand tighten. He added, "And Laurie Drake."

"It's always the young ones," Joan whispered.

"I don't think so," Ryerson said. "I don't think age matters. I think it's all in the soul."

She smiled. "You surprise me."

"With talk of the soul? I don't mean to."

"I got the clear idea that you were . . . antireligious."

He smiled, turned his head slightly to look at her. "I'm not antireligious, Joan. I have my beliefs, like everyone else."

"I'm glad to hear it."

"Yes," he said, "I know you are."

She let go of his hand suddenly. "I don't think I could ever get used to that, Rye."

"Get used to what?" he asked, feigning ignorance.

"You know very well what. That . . . habit you have of looking into people's heads whenever you want."

He took her hand; she resisted a little, then gave in. "It's not as simple as that, Joan. You of all people should know that. And I don't *look into* anyone's head. Whatever I see comes to me unsolicited, and most of what I see—God, most of it is best left unseen! You'd be surprised how many of our thoughts are . . ." He searched for the right word.

"Nasty?" Joan offered.

He smiled. "I was going to say 'inappropriate.' It's the academic in me, I guess. 'Nasty' is better." A short pause. "This . . . thing I'm looking at now is nasty." Another pause. "I tried to talk to him, Joan. He's right in the middle of it—"

"Who? Captain Lucas?"

Ryerson nodded. "Yes. Captain Lucas. Yesterday morning, he threw me out of his office. Then I went looking for him this morning—" He stopped.

"Rye?" Joan coaxed. "What's wrong?"

Ryerson said nothing.

"Rye, please."

"I don't know. I don't know. Something's not right here."

"Something's not right *where*? What in the hell are you talking about."

"Here, Joan." He looked earnestly at her. "In this house."

"Jesus, Rye—you're scaring the hell out of me."

"Yes, I know. I'm sorry." He shook his head; he was clearly agitated. "Joan, you've got to leave here, you've got to leave this house."

In the Buffalo Police Department Records Division

Glen Coffman said, "What was that shriek I heard? It sounded like someone goosed you."

Irene Sabitch looked over at him, a huge smile on her face. "I got it, Glen."

"Well, for heaven's sake, don't give it to me."

"I got into those damned files. I found the user number and I got into them. I asked myself, now, what number would I use if I were Captain Lucas. And I answered myself, hell, there could be any of a number of different combinations, but the most likely combination would probably reflect my ego. My birth date, my shield number, my telephone number. So I got hold of all the numbers associated with him—at least all the numbers I could find, and I've been imputting them for the last two days." She paused.

"And?" Glen coaxed.

"And, at last, I got it. Two-one-five, that's the date of the Curtis murder/suicide. February fifteenth. So, two one five point LUC, for Lucas. It wasn't very inventive, but I guess that was the beauty of it—someone like me nosing about would probably discard the obvious. And I did, until the *un*obvious didn't work."

Glenn said nothing for a moment; he was surprised. Then, "Congratulations; you may yet learn to be a computer operator." He got up, studied her monitor a moment, then looked confusedly at her. "Well, c'mon, where is it, where's the readout?"

"That's it," she said.

"That's it? That's the whole thing?" He was looking at three sets of numbers, one on top of the other. They read:

5556892
843
28910

"That's it," Irene said. "Every file contains only those three numbers. My guess was that this one"—she pointed at the top number—"was a phone number."

"Try it," Glen said.

"I did. I had the computer check it." She paused.

"Well, go on," Glen said impatiently. "What is this, suspense night in Records Division? What did the computer say?"

"It said that that was the number for Greyhound Package Express, on Peacock Street, ten years ago."

Chapter Eighteen

At 1:15 that afternoon, two bodies, a male and a female, were discovered at the home of Frank and Lilian Janus. The bodies were discovered by the couple's housekeeper, Mrs. Glassman, who spent no time examining them and had to be sedated when the authorities arrived a half hour later. Captain Jack Lucas, Detective Guy Mallory, and Detective Andrew Spurling were among those on the scene.

Captain Lucas bent over the female; she was on her back, and was dressed in a pink vest, pink skirt, and white Naturalizers. There was no clear evidence of the cause of death, although from her open mouth and eyes, her dilated pupils, and the pale light blue cast of her skin, she clearly was dead. Lucas said, "Where are the lab boys, dammit? I want to get this one turned over."

Mallory, who was kneeling near Frank Janus, said, "Hey, this guy's been shaved."

Detective Spurling stood by quietly, taking notes. Mallory said to him, "You okay, Andy?"

Spurling continued taking notes.

"Andy?" Mallory coaxed.

He looked up, smiled a little. "Yeah? What's the problem?"

"Are you all right?"

"Why wouldn't I be?"

"No reason; I guess you look a little ... removed."

"Double shift," Spurling explained. "I can handle it."

Lucas called, "Mallory, come here."

Mallory went over to Captain Lucas. Lucas asked, "If I got the name right, this is the woman who was attacked on Baldridge Street."

Mallory looked over at a uniformed cop standing near the doorway. "What's the name here, McGuire?" he asked.

McGuire answered, "Janus," spelled it, nodded at the body on the bed. "Her name was Lilian." He nodded at the body on the floor. "His was Frank. They were married, they had three kids, all in school. The two youngest are due home soon, I think."

Mallory turned back to Lucas. "She's the one, Captain."

Lucas straightened. "Help me turn her, Guy."

Mallory balked. "Don't you think we should wait for—"

"Help me turn her, goddammit."

Mallory sighed, came forward, stood next to Lucas, and together they turned the body of the female just enough that they could get a good look at her back. It was all but nonexistent. Where a wide flat plane of skin should have been, there was a gaping hole; at the edges of the hole were the broken and splintered ends of ribs, and within the hole a random jumble of internal organs. Covering these splintered bones and jumbled organs, softly reflecting the glow of the ceiling light, was the same creamy substance that had covered Laurie Drake. "Jesus Christ!" Mallory breathed, and covered his nose against the bittersweet smell of it.

Lucas said calmly, "Well, there's your cause of death, Mallory," and they let the body down.

Mallory said, "But where are the bandages, Captain?"

"What's that, a joke?" Lucas growled.

Mallory shook his head. "No," he said, "I'm sorry. You don't understand. The woman who was attacked on Baldridge Street had the entire side of her face ripped away." He nodded at the body on the bed. "And there's nothing wrong with *her* face, Captain."

Benny Bloom was very concerned. "What do you mean, Carlotta's in the psychiatric wing? I just talked to her yesterday."

The nurse who had taken Nurse Scotti's place was a chunky, gray-haired woman of sixty who affected a gentle and motherly bedside manner that Benny found annoying. She answered, "Nurse Scotti will be fit as a fiddle before you know it, Benny." She gave him her version of a sly grin. "It seems you've developed something of a crush on our pretty nurse. Ah, Benny, boys your age—"

"What's wrong with her?" Benny cut in, taking her by surprise—few people ever interrupted her sweet pontifications.

Her sly grin changed to a motherly, caring smile as she cooed, "Benny, Benny, your pretty nurse just needs a little rest; and so do you."

Benny shot back, "No, I don't," swung his feet over the bed to the floor, and went on brusquely. "Where is she? Where's the psychiatric wing?"

The chunky nurse's caring smile stuck on her face; she put her unusually strong hands on Benny's chest and tried to push him firmly but gently back onto the bed. "Ah, Benny," she cooed, "please be a good boy—"

And with his free right arm—his left was swathed in bandages—he gave her a mammoth shove that sent her stumbling backward toward the doorway, a sudden look of surprise and fear on her face. But she missed the doorway by an inch; her right side slammed into the wall, her head flew back, whiplash style, connected solidly with the metal doorjamb, and for a few moments she stood nearly motionless, arms quivering, mouth open, that look of surprise and fear mingling now with a look of motherly concern, as if her child had just shaken his fist at her or told her he was going to run away. "Ah, Benny," she managed, "look what you've done now." And she slid to the floor so she was in a sitting position, legs wide, arms at her sides, palms up, fingers curled, eyes and mouth open.

Benny cocked his head and looked quizzically at her. "What are you doing?" he asked.

Her mouth closed, opened, closed, opened. Small gurgling sounds came from her.

Benny cocked his head the other way. "Are you hurt?" he asked. A sudden scorching pain ripped into his belly; he doubled over. "No," he whispered. "Please, no!"

At that same moment, at the home of Lilian and Frank Janus, Captain Jack Lucas was saying, "Jesus, this is making me sick."

"Yeah," said Detective Mallory, "tell me about it."

"I mean it," Lucas said. "I gotta get outa here," and he pushed his way out of the Janus's bathroom, through the bedroom, and into the hallway.

In the bathroom Guy Mallory adjusted the blanket that covered Lilian Janus to her neck. She was in the fetal position; her thumb was in her mouth; the bandages at the side of her face had been torn halfway off—probably, Mallory supposed, by the woman herself—revealing the dead white skin beneath. The woman's open eyes were glazed over, as if by a nictitating membrane, although as he watched her, Mallory could see them move occasionally, as if she were watching a dream play itself out.

Mallory shook his head. "What the hell is going on here?" he asked no one in particular.

And Detective Andrew Spurling, standing in the bathroom doorway, said, "Captain's getting a little squeamish in his old age." He chuckled.

Mallory turned his head, fixed him with a stern gaze. "Haven't you got something to do, Detective?" he said.

Spurling, looking offended, answered in a tone of ill-disguised surliness, "You talking to me?"

"What did you say?" Mallory barked; he and Spurling were friends, after a fashion. They'd downed a few beers together, had bullshitted together, and their relationship was usually casual and cooperative. Mallory, however, had a very well developed sense of command, and Spurling's sudden change in attitude had taken him by surprise.

Spurling answered, "I *asked* if you were talking to me. If you *were* talking to me, *Ser*geant Mallory, then you'd best show a little respect."

Mallory was very quick. He stepped forward, grabbed Spurling by the collar, lifted him so he was on his tiptoes, and growled, "If you *ever* talk to me like that again, Detective, not only will I see to it that you're busted to patrolman, but I will personally break your jaw. Do you understand that? Nod once if you do."

Spurling hesitated, then nodded reluctantly. Mallory let go of his collar. "Good," he said, "now go and do whatever it is you were hired to do." He looked past Spurling at Officer McGuire. "McGuire, where the hell is the damned ambulance?"

And McGuire, who lately seemed to have lots of answers, responded, "It's just parking out front now, Sergeant."

Ryerson Biergarten asked the same desk sergeant he'd talked to the previous morning, "What call is Captain Lucas on? Where?"

And the sergeant, smiling, answered, "What are you going to do—go and watch?"

Ryerson took a breath, counted to three silently, then said, calling up his most authoritarian tones, "This is a matter of life and death, Sergeant. If you don't cooperate with me—" He stopped. When he went on a moment later, his authoritarian tone had changed to one of urgency. "Where on Ormond Street is he? What number?"

The sergeant was flabbergasted. "I—I never said anything . . ." He turned to the uniformed cops behind him. "Hey, you guys are witnesses, I never said anything to him about where the captain is; you'll vouch for me, right?"

The uniformed cops, a half-dozen of them, all looked up in unison, and confusion.

"Never mind," Ryerson said, "I know where to find him." And, with Creosote tucked under his arm, he went to his Woody, parked in front of the station, and drove north, toward Ormond Street, and the house where Lilian and Frank Janus used to live.

"Spurling?" called Guy Mallory from the bathroom of the Janus house; two ambulance attendants had just lifted Lilian Janus onto a stretcher. "Coming through," said the lead man, and Mallory stepped out of their way, into the bedroom. "Spurling?" he called again.

Officer McGuire, standing guard near the bedroom door, offered, "He left a few minutes ago, Sergeant."

"He left a few minutes ago?" Mallory was incredulous. "Did he say where in the hell he was going?"

McGuire nodded. "Yes, sir. He had to use the john downstairs, sir."

"Uh-huh," Mallory said. "And how about Captain Lucas?"

"He left the house, sir."

Mallory fumed, "What is this—the Keystone Kops?"

"Yes, sir," McGuire said.

"Are you trying to be funny, Officer?"

"No, sir."

Mallory nodded at Frank Janus's naked body in front of the bed. "Cover that, would you, McGuire," he said.

"Forensics hasn't been through here yet, sir."

Mallory rolled his eyes. "Everyone's an expert!" he whispered.

"Yes, sir," McGuire said.

There were several people in the room—a police photographer who was stepping gingerly around to line up shots, a technician just beginning to dust everything in the room for fingerprints, a woman kneeling over what had been incorrectly presumed to be the corpse of Lilian Janus; the woman had a small glass specimen holder in one hand and what looked like a flat-bladed scalpel in the other; she was scraping the inside of the corpse's left arm with it.

"Uh, miss?" Mallory said.

McGuire offered, "She's with the M.E.'s office, Sergeant."

"I'll ask the questions, McGuire."

"Yes, sir."

The woman looked around at Mallory. "I *am* with the Medical Examiner's Office, Detective."

"Okay," Mallory said, "but would you mind telling me what the hell you're doing? You've got the body—what in God's name would you need with—"

"They're fresh," the woman said, smiling an apology for interrupting him. "The scrapings are fresh tissue, more or less. It's going to be another hour, maybe two, before the M.E. starts his autopsy, and by then this body will be well into the process of degeneration. Cellular structure is very fragile, Detective, especially if you intend to do the kinds of tests with it that we think are going to be required. What we've got here is something very, very strange."

Spurling appeared in the doorway and stopped next to McGuire. McGuire said, "Yes, sir," and Spurling looked confusedly at him; then he grinned, pleased. "You're a good man, McGuire," he said.

"Yes, sir," McGuire said, and the heel of his foot hit the floor.

Mallory called sharply, "You're not in the army here, McGuire. Loosen up."

"Yes, sir," McGuire said.

"And cut out the damned 'yes sirs' and 'no sirs.'"

"Certainly," McGuire said.

Spurling said, "There's some bozo downstairs looking for Captain Lucas."

Chapter Nineteen

Ryerson, standing on the sidewalk halfway to the front porch steps at the Janus home, was fighting to maintain some appearance of composure and normalcy.

It was a difficult fight, but so far he was winning it.

Most of those around him were uniformed cops. Pat Farrel, the reporter for the *Buffalo Evening News*, was there, too, waiting impatiently for word from someone on what was going on. "Mr. Biergarten," he'd said when Ryerson had appeared at the house and had asked one of the uniforms if he could see Captain Lucas, "what would interest a psychic investigator here? Does this have something to do with that 'psychic storm' you talked about two days ago?" and Ryerson had been forced by what he was seeing to ignore him.

The Janus home was in a fashionable west side neighborhood. It was a big, cedar-sided contemporary house surrounded by similar houses. The lawn was elegantly manicured, the landscaping a tad ostentatious, though not overbearing, and the whole effect was one of calculated neatness, and taste.

But that was not all that Ryerson was seeing.

He was also seeing demons.

Demons slavering at the windows; demons slithering through doors; demons poking their awful heads from the chimney; demons squatting beneath the shrubs.

And for Ryerson, the really hellish thing of it all was this: he knew that these demons were real. As real as the house, as real as the grass, as real as his damned argyle socks.

As real as Joan believed them to be.

Murderously, obscenely real!

They were not merely something that his incredibly sensitive and creative psyche had manufactured to give his *feelings* palpability—something to touch and hold on to because feelings all by themselves can slip away in an instant. That had happened before; his mind's eye had created for him what his feelings told him were real. In Boston, at a house plagued by classic poltergeist-type hauntings, he had seen the grinning head of a young girl bouncing like a basketball from room to room, and from that was able to link the hauntings to a girl of twelve who lived at the house. But that bouncing head had not been real, and he knew it the moment he saw it. It was a symbol, a representation of reality. He'd been certain of that right from the start.

His only certainty now, in front of the Janus house, was that the world was alive with possibilities. Crawling, slithering, slavering, grinning possibilities.

"Hey," he heard one of the uniformed cops nearby say, though to Ryerson it sounded as if the cop were a million miles away, "you wanta move back a little; this is a crime scene, you know."

Ryerson took no notice of him.

The demons he was seeing were much as he would have imagined them. They were thin and misshapen, fat and smooth and wrinkled, olive-colored and dull orange and very light blue; they were translucent, transparent, beaked, fanged, owl-eyed and eyeless; they crawled, they hopped, they hunkered about on thin greasy thighs; they were monkey-faced, no-faced, two-faced, motionless; they vibrated like water, they sang, they hooted, they were shrill the way bluejays are shrill; they sat on necks, on arms, on heads, their huge crooked organs dangling over noses and mouths; they smelled of the earth, and of death, and of winter air.

They were as present as air.

The uniformed cop said again, "Get *out* of the way, mister—this is a *crime* scene!"

"Who the hell is he?" said another one.

"He's looking for Captain Lucas."

Ryerson began to lose it. His body quivered; his mouth opened and closed; his eyes watered from staying open too long.

Guy Mallory appeared in front of him. He said, "Captain Lucas isn't here. I'll tell him you were looking for him. What'd you say your name was?"

"Uhn . . . uhn," said Ryerson.

"I didn't quite catch that," Mallory said.

Ryerson closed his eyes tightly. "Uhn . . . uhn," he said again.

"Jesus Christ, get a hold of yourself," Mallory said.

"Rye," said a woman's voice. "Rye? Come with me. Come away from here."

Ryerson felt, very distantly, a slight pressure on his arm.

"Who are you?" Mallory asked.

"My name's Joan Mott Evans. I'm a friend of Mr. Biergarten's."

"You mean this is Ryerson Biergarten, the psychic? It was my understanding that Captain Lucas—"

"I don't care what your understanding was," Joan said.

Ryerson opened his eyes. "Must leave," he whispered.

"That's my idea exactly," Joan said.

He shook his head firmly. "No, all of us must leave here. Now!"

"What's he, nuts?" Mallory said.

"No," Joan answered, "he's psychic. He sees things."

"We all have our little crosses to bear," Mallory said.

"Leave!" Ryerson yelled. "All of you, leave this house now! Burn it, burn the whole neighborhood—get away from here!"

Joan tugged firmly on his arm. "C'mon, Rye. We'll take your car; I'll come back for mine later."

Ryerson let himself be led to the Woody. Joan opened the passenger door. He looked back. He could see that he had everyone's attention now. The cops, Pat Farrel, the neighbors who had gathered in a rough semi-circle around the house. And the others.

The ones perched on heads and chimneys; the ones who hung out of windows; the ones with organs dangling in front of human noses; the ones who were translucent, burnt orange, owl-eyed and eyeless.

And all of them were grinning at him.

We've won, their grins said.

"Get *out*!" Ryerson screamed. "Get out, get out, get out . . ." And Joan pushed him into the passenger seat of the Woody, ran around to the driver's door, and climbed in.

"Get out!" Ryerson screamed through the open window.

The others continued to grin at him.

"Keys," Joan said. "Rye, give me the keys."

"You must leave," Ryerson screamed.

"Please, you must leave!" he pleaded with the people around the Janus house.

"Dammit, Rye, give me the keys!"

"For your own sake, for the sake of your city—"

Joan reached across the seat, took hold of his right lapel, and yanked hard on it so he turned his head to look at her. "Give me the keys!" she demanded.

He looked blankly at her for several moments, as if he didn't recognize her, then he whispered, "Yes, of course, the keys," and he fished them from his pocket and gave them to her. Seconds later they were on their way back to her house.

Benny Bloom leaned over Nurse Carlotta Scotti, asleep in her room in the psychiatric wing of Buffalo Memorial Hospital. He whispered, "I'm not myself lately, Carlotta." He paused, smiled, went on. "But I know that I love you, and that I need you and want you."

Carlotta did not awaken. She was in the deep and dreamless sleep that sedation brings.

Benny cooed on. "We can be very happy together, Carlotta. You and I can be very, very happy together."

Behind him, a graceful feminine hand reached around the edge of the doorway. Then a pair of large and sensuous brown eyes peered into the room and quickly summed up what was happening in it; a pair of full red lips parted in a smile of recognition. And the mind behind the eyes said, *Yes, yes, this is one of us!*

Benny Bloom heard an earthy other-side-of-the-tracks voice. "Come on over here," it said. "You want a good time, you come on over here!"

Benny turned his head quickly from Carlotta, saw the woman in the doorway. He scowled. "Go away," he said. "You're disturbing us."

Benny was Benny then.

Benny was always Benny. The nerd who was the darling of the high honor roll crowd was Benny. The jock who quoted T. S. Eliot was Benny, too. He was stronger, cockier, meaner, but he was Benny. So the entity within him, the entity which had invaded his body five days earlier, did not have to work very hard. The Benny it invaded was also the Benny who turned and faced Carlotta Scotti, and he had the same eyes, the same nose, the same chin, legs, arms, and body. But he was oh so obscenely different from the Benny she had gotten to know, the Benny she had been nursing back to health. Because some changes do not have to stretch the bones and muscles.

But it was not the same with the creature beckoning to him from the doorway. She was a fabrication, a piece of murderous manufacture—just as Loni had been, just as the murderer of bad-check-writer Warren Anderson had been, just as the woman who stuck a knife through Frank Janus's heart had been. Because what slumbers inside us sometimes *does* stretch the bone and muscle.

Now that creature, that piece of murderous manufacture, stepped into Carlotta Scotti's room, crossed it with amazing quickness and grace, and faced Benny, while in the bed behind him, Nurse Scotti stirred in her sleep: she was rising from the silent depths where the sedative had taken her, and dreams were pushing into her brain.

Something stirred then in Benny, too. Awareness, need, recognition. His stomach quivered as the woman facing him bared her breasts, pulled his hospital gown up, and rubbed her cool, hard nipples against the hot skin of his chest. "Oh Jesus, oh God," he breathed.

And the woman whispered at him, "Hey, honey, those two don't have nothin' to do with this." A wide smile parted her lips. She grabbed his erect penis with her right hand, and with her left she reached around and caressed his buttocks. She whispered, "C'mon now, Benny, push it in, bend down a little"—he did—"and push it in. That's right. That's good. Oh, damn, Benny, that's so good!"

"Creosote's sick," Ryerson said. The dog was asleep on his lap, its breathing shallow and irregular.

Joan, seated next to Ryerson on the couch, said, "What did you see at that house, Rye? Please tell me."

He shook his head. "I don't know what I saw, Joan." A short pause. "I saw demons. I don't believe in demons, but I saw demons there."

Joan nodded. "Yes, I saw them, too."

He looked questioningly at her.

She explained, "I saw *some*thing, Rye. I saw shadows." A pause. "I saw moving shadows."

He looked away. "I—I don't . . ." he stammered.

"No," she said. "I don't understand it, either."

He smiled. "You're getting pretty good at this, Joan."

"I don't welcome it," she said.

Ryerson stood, Creosote cradled in his arms. "I'd like you to stay here, Joan. At the house. Please don't come looking for me; I think you'll be much safer here."

"Do you know how paternal and sexist that sounds, Rye? *Who* had to rescue *whom* today?"

He grinned at her. "You're right, of course. I'm sorry. But I would still like you to stay here. And please don't ask why."

"Why?" she said.

He sighed. "Why should you stay here? Or why shouldn't you ask why you should stay here?"

"You're a real card, Ryerson Biergarten. This isn't some grade B western, and I'm not some quivering southern belle who needs to be protected from . . . from whatever it is"

—she waved at the air—"that you want to protect me from. I'm an adult, I'm smart, I'm strong, and I'm fully capable of taking care of myself."

Ryerson hesitated; something cold and threatening had just passed through him. He shook his head, tried to get it back because he wanted to look at it, wanted to examine it, and find its focus. But it was gone. He grinned at Joan, feigned a casual shrug, and said, "Well, I really wasn't intimating anything at all—"

"Oh, c'mon, Rye—you were too. Now, I know that you're going to take Creosote to the vet. But I don't know where you're going after that."

Ryerson sighed. "To a bar called Frank's Place," he answered.

"Okay," she said. "I could use a drink."

An hour later Ryerson had, reluctantly, given Creosote over for the night to Dr. Craig Gibson, D.V.M. "I'll run some tests on him, Mr. Biergarten," Gibson explained. "I suspect an allergy."

"Do what you feel is necessary," Ryerson had said, then, after assuring Creosote that he wasn't abandoning him, that he'd be back the next day, he went, with Joan, to Frank's Place.

Chapter Twenty

Officer Leonard McGuire appeared from within the Janus kitchen and motioned to Guy Mallory, standing in the foyer with the woman from the Medical Examiner's Office. The woman said to Mallory, whose attention was on her, "I think that cop wants to talk to you," and nodded at McGuire.

Mallory looked over at him. "Yeah, what is it, McGuire?"

"There's some trouble at the hospital, Sergeant," McGuire answered.

"What hospital?"

"Buffalo Memorial, sir."

"What kind of trouble?"

McGuire looked mystified. "What *kind* of trouble, sir?" He paused; his look of mystification grew stronger. "I don't know, sir. All I know is they've got trouble there. I don't know what kind of trouble it is."

Two morgue attendants came down the stairs carrying the body of Frank Janus on a stretcher. "Step aside, please," said the lead man, and Mallory and the woman from the M.E.'s office moved out of the foyer, closer to McGuire. McGuire backed quickly away from them.

Mallory asked him, "What are you—nervous?"

"No, sir," he answered.

"Well, you look nervous; you look like you've got ants in your pants."

"No, sir. I'm only doing my job, sir."

Mallory grimaced. "I asked you before not to call me 'sir.'"

McGuire nodded quickly, stiffly. "Yes. Certainly."

Mallory studied McGuire's face closely, then said, "Listen, I think you're having a rough time of it here. Why don't you go back to the station, fill out your report, and call it a day."

McGuire clicked his heel on the floor. "Yes, sir." He saluted.

Mallory shook his head resignedly. "Go on now," he said, "get outa here. And take the long way back if you want; collar a few jaywalkers, run down a few speeders. I think you could use a break from all this crap, Officer McGuire."

"Yes, sir," McGuire barked, and with another click of the heel, and another salute, he moved quickly past them, through the foyer, around the men bearing the stretcher down the sidewalk, to his squad car. He got in, slammed the door, fired up the engine, and roared away from the curb.

Mallory turned to the woman from the M.E.'s office. "Jesus," he said, "that man's on a ragged edge for sure."

And the woman from the M.E.'s office said, "That man should be given an immediate leave of absence, Detective. If you ask me, he's on the verge of a breakdown."

All his life Leonard McGuire wanted only to do what he was told to do because that made life easier for him. At home his father took all of Leonard's decision-making on his own shoulders because, he assured Leonard, "you certainly can't make decisions yourself." And in school Leonard, who was not at all stupid, did precisely what he was told by his teachers and made it through twelve grades with hassles to no one. Then, several years after getting out of the Marines, he was hired by the Buffalo Police Department. And, much to his surprise, he found that he could make decisions. Most of them were right; some of them weren't. And after a while, the ones that weren't began to turn the tide, began to convince him yet again that, as his father said, he didn't have the brains that God gave geese. Then his decisions became momentous and nerve-jarring, and he longed to have them made for him.

Then he was there in "The District" when Detective Third Grade Andrew Spurling launched himself into the abandoned tank tread factory, there at the ready with a flashlight, there when the beam of the flashlight fell on that incredibly beautiful and hungry woman.

There when she put her mouth first on Spurling, then on Mathilde, then on him. There when she stepped back from them and proclaimed, "You have so much life in you, so much life in you!"

And that's when he began to change. When he began to revert to what he knew, deep in his heart, was the only thing he could be—a programmable cop.

Collar a jaywalker, he'd been told. *Run down a speeder*, he'd been told.

The middle-aged woman on Greeley Place glanced at her speedometer; it read thirty-five. Wasn't that the speed limit? She glanced about, saw a speed limit sign. It read thirty. "Oh, heavens," she muttered, and realized sinkingly that the cop behind her was indeed stopping her, not someone else, not, for instance, those awful motorcycle hoodlums who'd passed her a few minutes before.

She pulled her Dodge Diplomat over to the curb, brought it to a jarring halt because she was nervous—it was the first time she'd been stopped in nearly forty years of driving, a fact she intended to share quite vocally with the policeman who'd stopped her.

She glanced around at the patrol car parked a good two car lengths behind her, saw the cop sitting behind the wheel, and stared at him a few moments. She decided he was probably "running a make" (as they said on the TV cop shows) on her license number and would be getting out of his car momentarily. She opened her purse, dug around in her Kleenex mini-tissues, her lipsticks, compacts, receipts, loose change, and other assorted odds and ends until she came up with her wallet. She got her license from it, studied it closely to be sure it hadn't expired. It hadn't. She sighed, relieved, opened the glove box, and poked around in the profusion of junk in there until she found her insurance card. Then, happy that all her paperwork seemed to be in order, she glanced out her side window, thinking that surely the cop would be standing next to the car by now. But he wasn't. She glanced back at his car, saw that he was still behind the wheel, and that there was a strange fixed stare in his eyes. She put her hand on the door handle. She hesitated, sensed that something was not quite right. Then she opened her door and stepped out onto the pavement.

The last sound she heard was the roar of the patrol car's big V-8 as it sprang to life.

* * *

The bartender at Frank's Place said to Ryerson Biergarten, "I see you traded in your little dog for a better model," and nodded to indicate Joan.

Ryerson said, "I don't understand."

The bartender shrugged. "What's to understand? I was making a joke."

"Oh," Ryerson said, pretending a smile, "a joke. I see. You were drawing some parallel between my dog and this woman? Is that what you were doing?"

"Rye," Joan said, "it's okay. Forget it."

The bartender shook his head. "No. Like the lady says, forget it. What'll you have?"

"What I'll have first is an apology," Ryerson said.

And Joan said, "It's not necessary. Really. It was just a joke. You don't have to protect me."

"Okay," warned the bartender, "if you came in here to make trouble, mister—"

Ryerson cut in, "Why did you break your sister's arm?"

"Huh?" said the bartender, flabbergasted.

"It was a clear enough question," Ryerson said. "When you were fifteen, you broke your little sister's arm. Why?"

"You fucking lousy bastard—"

"Where's Jack Lucas?"

"Jack Lucas? I don't know no Jack Lucas. I told you that before."

"You were lying."

The bartender bristled. "No one calls me a liar—"

"Jack ain't here," said a voice from the opposite end of the bar. Ryerson looked over. He saw the woman, Doreen, who'd been there the last time he'd been in Frank's Place. He started for her; Joan took his arm, stopped him. "What in the hell are you doing, Rye?"

He glanced at her; she saw confusion, frustration, and anger in his eyes. He said, "I'm not sure, Joan. I've got to find Jack Lucas. I don't know why, but I've got to find him. And please don't ask me to explain my actions. I don't think I could—I do what I have to do." And with that, he went to the end of the bar to talk to the woman who called herself Doreen. Joan sat at a table nearby.

The woman said, as Ryerson sat on a barstool next to her, "We got trouble in this city, don't we, Mr. Biergarten?"

It was a question he had not anticipated.

Benny Bloom had very vague memories of coming here—wherever *here* was. He saw himself standing over Carlotta Scotti, heard himself talking to her, telling her how much he loved her and how much he needed her.

He remembered the sensuous woman who had glided over to him across Carlotta's room, remembered that she had put her hands on him, and he had put his hands on her, that she had made him feel very, very good.

And he remembered coming here. Remembered being put in the backseat of a big black car, remembered something cagelike about that backseat, remembered the wail of sirens.

Then he was put here. In this big, damp cement-block building whose windows were high on the walls, where girders snaked about and the smell of urine and feces was heavy in the air.

And now as he looked about he could see that there were others here, too. Some of them were still, as if sleeping, and others moaned pitifully, and still others stood as he watched, and shivered as if from cold.

"That's what I hear, Mr. Biergarten," Doreen said, and took a long slug of her water glass full of whiskey. She put the glass down hard on the bar as if for emphasis. "I hear we got big trouble in this city."

Ryerson asked, "What did you say your name was?"

She smiled, revealing a mouth full of gleaming white teeth behind full red lips. "My name's Doreen, Mr. Biergarten—"

Ryerson cut in, "How did you know my name?"

Two men came into the bar. One was big and surly-looking; the other was smaller, balding, but somehow just as surly-looking.

They sat at the opposite end of the bar. Doreen said, "I know lots of things, Mr. Biergarten. Besides, I read the papers like everyone else."

"Good for you," Ryerson said.

"Ryerson H. Biergarten," Doreen announced. "Psychic Detective! I'm very impressed. We're all of us here very, very impressed." She drained what was left in the glass of whiskey, held it up for the bartender to see, nodded at it. He came over, filled it again from a nearly empty bottle of Five Star. "What's the *H* stand for, Mr. Biergarten. 'Hell-raiser'?" She hooted suddenly with a strange, low-pitched masculine kind of laughter that crept under Ryerson's skin and made him shiver.

And when he shivered, and as she laughed, the field of blue that had been with him these past five days, like a summer rash altered, grew indistinct, and for barely a moment was gone.

A hive took its place. A hive made up of a thousand, ten thousand, one hundred thousand bees—workers and drones, all moving furiously in attendance to the queen, who sat huge and resplendent at the center of the living, moving mass of bees. Then the image was gone, the field of blue returned, and Doreen said, "You look like you been seein' things, Mr. Biergarten." The ghost of a grin passed across her mouth. "You been seein' things, have you?" Another small grin flickered, and was gone.

"Queen bee," Ryerson said to no one in particular.

And at the table nearby, Joan echoed him: "Queen bee."

Detective Andrew Spurling thought he had never felt so good. He wished, vaguely, that he knew *why* he felt so good, that he could put a finger on it and say *Yes, I feel good because* . . . But he couldn't. Not that it mattered much, he decided—simply feeling good was enough.

He knocked on the door of Room 12 at the Do-Right Motel, off Route 16, three miles north of Buffalo. From within the room a female voice answered, "Yes? Who is it?"

"Police, ma'am," Spurling answered.

There was silence.

"Open up, please," Spurling called.

"Can you tell me why?" the woman called back.

"Yes, ma'am. It's about a bad check."

"Bad check? I didn't write any bad check. What in the hell are you talking about?"

"Whether you know—" Spurling began, and put his hand to his stomach against the surge of pain there. "Whether you know what I'm talking about or not—" Another surge of pain; it came and went quickly. He looked down at his feet, smiled; his pants cuffs were inching toward the tips of his shoes. "Whether you know or not—"

The woman called, "You're not a cop. Who the hell are you?"

Spurling looked at the window to his left. He saw that the woman was holding the mauve curtain aside and peering out at him, stark confusion on her face. As he watched, her look of confusion became one of fear and bewilderment. He pulled his .38 from his shoulder holster, saw the woman look agape at it, saw the window shatter as the bullet tore through it, saw the right side of the woman's neck disintegrate, saw the woman fall backward. Then the mauve curtain hid her.

And from behind him, he heard, "What in the name of God—"

His eleven-year-old frame turned very quickly, despite the fact that it was swimming around inside a suit five sizes too large for it. He trained the .38 on a tall, gray-haired man wearing a blue vest and cream-colored pants. He said, "No one messes with Andy Spurling no more!" He fired. The man crumpled to the pavement. And as he crumpled, Spurling lifted the barrel of the .38 and blew away the smoke curling raggedly from it.

Chapter Twenty-One

Benny Bloom said to a thin, dark-haired woman in her early twenties who was seated near him on the cold cement floor, her legs straight, arms hanging loosely, head back, "What is this place? Where are we?"

The woman, dressed as if for gardening, in bib overalls and a ragged long-sleeved shirt, turned her head slowly toward him. The barest whisper of a smile creased her face; it was a face that spoke eloquently of weariness and resignation. She said, "You're new. You don't know. This is where she keeps us."

"She?"

"When we're ourselves," the woman said, "this is where she keeps us."

Benny shook his head. "No, please, you don't understand—who is 'she'? Who are you talking about?"

"The woman."

"The woman? What woman?"

A piercing scream, a scream of incredible pain, filled the huge room, and a grunt of surprise escaped Benny. He turned his head quickly toward the source of the scream. He saw little, only the half-dozen or so people in the room, a few of them, like this woman, seated wearily against the wall, one, a young man, was walking aimlessly about; at the far end of the room, another young man lay flat on his back, arms wide, legs together, as if he were on a cross—asleep, Benny assumed. He turned anxiously to the young woman seated near him. "What was that scream?" he asked.

"That is what happens to some of us," she answered. "It will happen to me before long; I can feel it." She said this with no particular emotion, as if she were telling him that eventually she'd need glasses, or that eventually she'd get liver spots.

Benny shook his head briskly, in disbelief and fear. "What *is* this place?" he pleaded.

"It's where she keeps us," the woman answered. "When we're ourselves, it's where she keeps us."

Ryerson wasn't sure how long Joan had been staring fixedly at the woman who called herself Doreen. He had sensed fear from her the moment they'd entered Frank's Place, so when he turned toward her and saw that fixed stare, and saw that her whole body was trembling, he supposed she could have been that way for quite some time, because his attention for the last ten minutes or so had been on Doreen.

He went over to Joan and put a comforting hand on her shoulder. "Joan?" he coaxed. "Are you all right?"

She shook her head. "No. I'm scared, Rye." A nod at Doreen. "She scares me."

"How? Tell me how she scares you, Joan."

Joan shook her head again. "I can't," she whispered, as if fearful Doreen would hear her. "I don't know—it's the same kind of fear that some people have when they turn a rock over and see a strange-looking insect underneath." She smiled quiveringly. "Rye, I've turned this particular rock over before."

Ryerson glanced quickly at Doreen, who was smiling in their direction, then back at Joan. "Joan," he said, "I'm supposed to be so damned psychic, but I haven't got the foggiest idea what you're talking about. Are you saying that you know this woman?"

"No. I don't know her. I've never seen her before." She took Ryerson's arm, coaxed him closer to her. "But Rye," she said, voice low, "she knows me. And she scares the hell out of me."

In the Buffalo Police Department Records Division

"We have to have a damned warrant," Irene Sabitch grumbled as she hung up the telephone receiver.

"Well, Jesus," Glen said, "I could have told you that."

She gave him a weary look. "I'm sure you could tell me quite a few things, Glen."

He held his hands up, palms out. "Don't shoot, don't shoot!" He smiled. She rolled her eyes. He went on. "So what are you going to do now?"

She sighed. "What can I do? Getting a warrant to look into a precinct captain's Greyhound Express locker would be like ... like ..." She was stumped.

Glen offered, "Like saying yes to going out with me, Irene?"

She nodded enthusiastically. "It would be at least that hard."

He looked crestfallen, though only for a moment. He smiled. "Can't blame me for trying."

"Uh-huh." A pause. "You know, Glen, Captain Lucas put those numbers there"—she nodded at her monitor—"for a reason. Hell, he told me not to meddle for a reason." She shrugged. "It's only a theory, but I think he *wants* to be caught, Glen."

"Sure, Irene. Sure," Glen said. "But caught at *what*?"

She looked blankly at him. "Gee," she said, "I don't know."

Officer Leonard McGuire glanced at his reflection in the rearview mirror. He could see his right eye, his eyebrow, part of his forehead. He said aloud, "Who am I looking at? Who are you?" The reflection stared back impassively.

He also wanted to know where he was going. Where, in reality, he was being *drawn*, and who or what was drawing him there.

He recognized the area he was in: "The District," where, several days earlier—and it seemed like centuries now—he and Mathilde and Spurling had found the body of a wino.

A call came over McGuire's radio: "All cars in the area of Bailey Avenue and Schyler respond to two one two"—hit and run—"white female. Suspect vehicle last seen heading north. Suspect vehicle is described as closely resembling a black and white unit."

McGuire grabbed his mike, hit the talk button, said, "Unit Fourteen respond—" And put the mike down.

The radio squawked back, "Unit Fourteen? Come in, Unit Fourteen."

He pulled the squad car over to the curb, stopped, pushed his door open, got out, turned stiffly, and faced the huge cement-block building to his right. Vaguely he was aware of the acrid stench of the smelters two miles away. Just as vaguely he was aware of a low humming noise from within the big cement building, as if there were people inside it. And very, very powerfully, he realized that he was being manipulated; that whatever had drawn him here would draw him into that building and then would do with him what it pleased.

But as powerfully as he realized this, he realized just as powerfully, just as hellishly, that there was absolutely nothing he could do about it.

Ryerson watched Joan leave Frank's Place. She'd told him to take all the time he needed but that she'd wait in the car. "I shouldn't have come here in the first place, Rye," she'd said. "I'm scared. That woman scares the hell out of me."

He turned to the woman; she was smiling at him, a coy smile that whispered of victory. He said to her, "How do you know Jack Lucas?"

"We're friends," she answered quickly and smoothly, as if she'd anticipated the question. "We go back—" Her smile broadened. "A long time."

"How long?"

She sipped her whiskey, reached into her bodice, withdrew a soiled hanky from it, and wiped the lipstick from her glass. "Months," she said.

"Months?" Ryerson said.

"Oh, yes," she said, "a long time."

"And how long have you known Miss Evans?"

She missed a step. A small half-step, but Ryerson noticed it. And when she missed it, the fog and static that he'd been reading from her lifted very briefly and he was able to peer past it.

He saw little.

Only an evening sky littered with stars. And, underlying it, the suggestion of a wire fence. And beyond the fence, a field of chickweed and clover.

He knew that he'd been there. He'd seen it from a slightly different angle, perhaps, and not very well, because his night vision was all but nonexistent. But he had been there.

If only he could remember when.

Then the fog settled and Doreen was back in step. "*Miss* Evans is imagining things, my man." Another sip of the whiskey, another swipe at the lipstick on the glass. "I don't like kids. Maybe *Miss* Evans does"—another coy smile appeared—" 'cuz some of us ain't too discriminatin'. But me, I like my meat well done." She gave Ryerson a long, critical once-over. "Yes, sir, very well done."

Her once-over made Ryerson very uncomfortable. He glanced nervously about at the two men at the opposite end of the bar, then at the bartender, who was clearly trying to look like he didn't give a damn what Ryerson did, then back at Doreen, who began to chuckle.

And as she chuckled, the fog and static he'd been reading from her lifted once again. Again he saw a sky crowded with stars, the hint of a wire fence, a field of chickweed and clover.

And he saw something else, too. Something that brought a gasp from him and made him step involuntarily away from her, as if from something obscene.

He saw the damp reddish-brown earth all around her as if it were some kind of bizarre halo.

And as he backed away from her, her chuckling quickened. "You got problems, Mr. Biergarten? You don't like Doreen?"

Chapter Twenty-Two

Joan had been asleep for only a few hours when the dream started, the same dream that had driven her screaming into wakefulness a dozen times before. She saw the field of chickweed and clover, the wire fence gleaming dully in the moonlight, and she knew that if she came up over the rise, she would see the spot where Lila had been buried, and the nightmare would have her in its grasp at last.

Already, she could feel that a clammy sweat had started, that a cold knot of panic had formed in her stomach.

So, as she had a dozen times before, she bit her lip hard to wake herself. And saw the field of chickweed and clover undulate, as if it were a reflection on a pond. Then the wire fence, gleaming in the moonlight, lost itself in infinity. And she knew that the awful grip of the dream was starting to fade.

She knew also that she had succeeded only in chasing it off yet again. That it would return until, as Ryerson had told her, "it has played itself out." And even as she woke she knew that her wisest course of action would be to let the dream do just that—play itself out. Complete the circle. "I do it with songs that get stuck in my head," Ryerson had also told her. "I force the song to complete itself, to come to an end. And when it does complete itself, I'm usually free of it."

"Usually?" she'd said.

"Nothing's perfect," he'd said.

But now, in darkness, with the tail end of the dream still in sight, she had no stomach for anything except to turn on the light, sit up in the bed, and get her mind on something else. If she woke Ryerson, too, that was okay.

She opened her eyes. "Rye?" she whispered tentatively, voice quivering. "Wake up, Rye." She reached for him. "Rye?" She turned her head, strained to see in the darkness. "Damn!" she said aloud. The other side of the bed was empty.

She swung her feet to the floor. "Damn!" she said again. She looked about the room, saw only the hulking, dark gray suggestion of the wing chair against the north wall, the chest of drawers near it, the bookcase against the opposite wall.

She saw also that the door to the living room stood open.

"Rye," she called, "are you out there?" and knew almost at once that he wasn't, that his all-but-nonexistent night vision did not allow him to walk around in darkness. And from what she could see through the doorway, the house was dark.

She turned on the bedside lamp. Its low-wattage bulb illuminated a small area around her and turned the rest of the room a dull yellow.

"Rye, are you—" she began, and stopped. Something had moved away from the open door.

Ryerson parked the Woody several blocks from Frank's Place, got out, closed the door softly, and began walking down the center of the narrow street. He sensed little life in the big cement-block buildings around him. Now and then, desperate pieces of drug-induced dreams slapped at him. Now and then, he felt eyes on him and he knew that they were not human eyes.

It was a little past 3:00, that time of the morning when the world is at its darkest; especially here, where the streetlamps had long since burned out, and a low mantle of clouds lay sullen and still overhead.

He walked in the center of the narrow street. He could see very little in darkness such as this, only the dark gray and shimmering geometry of the buildings flat against the black sky and the black pavement. He guessed that there were no hazards in the roadway. On the sidewalk there could be open doors, trash, perhaps even someone sleeping off a hangover, and if he saw any of these things at all, it would be when he was half a heartbeat away from falling over them. So he stuck to the middle of the street, where he could roughly gauge its edges.

He was going to Frank's Place to find Jack Lucas.

"Is that you, Rye?" Joan called, knowing that he probably wouldn't be sulking about in the darkened house. Still, the possibility—remote as it was—was something to cling to: "Don't play games with me, Rye," she called. "I need you." She smiled quickly. "I do need you, Rye. Come in here and hold me."

And a voice answered from the other room, "You'd like that, wouldn't you, Joan?"

Five miles away, on a darkened street, in the desolate and all-but-abandoned area of the city known as "The District," Ryerson Biergarten gasped, doubled over in pain, crumpled to his knees, got down on all fours. "No," he moaned, "for the love of God, no!" Then, despite the pain, he reared up on his knees, held his arms wide, clenched his fists. "Damn you!" he screamed. "Damn you! Damn you! Damn you!" Because he had realized at last where he had seen the field of chickweed and clover revealed to him when the woman who called herself Doreen had chuckled and her mind had opened up to him very briefly.

He had seen it six months earlier.

He had seen it in Edgewater. At the cemetery where Lila Curtis was buried.

He screamed again, "No! Oh my God, no!"

And from the edges of the buildings around him, a hundred pairs of eyes turned from the psychic storm brewing in the air around him.

Joan wanted to speak but couldn't. Her breathing was shallow and fast and the lack of oxygen was making her dizzy.

"Remember me, Joan?" teased the voice from the other room.

Joan found her voice briefly. "Go away," she pleaded.

"But Joan, I thought we were pals. Aren't we pals?"

"Go away," she whispered.

"No, no, no, Joan. I'm here to stay."

Ryerson hadn't gone far from the Woody, only a hundred feet or so, and, normally, finding his way back to it would have been easy. But not in darkness such as this. Not when his eyes were all but useless. In his panic and desperation, he'd gone right instead of making a 180-degree turn. And though he saw the vague, dirty cream-colored suggestion of the curb, he saw it too late, stumbled over it, and his forward momentum sent him headlong toward the wall only a few feet away. He thrust his hands out to cushion the impact. His arms buckled; he instinctively tucked his head. And hit the wall hard. First with his shoulder, then, spinning around from the momentum, with his back, and got the wind knocked out of him. He fell gasping to one knee, grabbed his shoulder. After what seemed like a very long time, his breathing normalized, he moaned one of his rare curses, and pushed himself to his feet. He stood quietly for a moment, trying to gauge his location. Around him the buildings, the street, and the sky blended into an undulating milky-gray sameness.

Then he sensed that there were eyes on him again. The same eyes that had been watching him since he'd gotten out of the Woody and started walking. The eyes of nocturnal predators and scavengers. Eyes that were easily a hundred times more sensitive than any man's. Eyes that he could use if only he could make the tiny brains behind them open up and communicate with him.

"Who are you?" Joan pleaded. "Please, who *are* you?"

"Oh, come on, Joan," said the voice in the other room. "You know me." Then, at the edges of the dull yellow light cast by her bedside lamp, she could see that something was moving with graceful and deliberate slowness toward her through the living room, and she screamed, "Who *are* you, goddammit, who *are* you?!"

She heard a chuckle, low and menacing, then another, and another and another, until they blended into a kind of loud rushing noise, like dirt falling on metal.

It ended abruptly.

Doreen appeared in her bedroom doorway. And smiled a huge seductive smile. And said, her voice dripping with apology, "I gotta hurt you, Joan. I gotta hurt you!"

Joan screamed, "I don't *know* you!"

"Course you don't. But I know you." She stuck two fingers into her ample cleavage.

"What . . . are you doing?" Joan stammered.

Doreen withdrew a small silver folding knife, held it up in front of her eyes, and snapped it open with a flick of the wrist. The blade was short, almost harmless-looking. Doreen whispered hoarsely, as if emotion were pinching her voice, "Don't look like much, does it, Joan? Hell, it ain't much, really. But let me ask you something; you ever seen what a cat can do with its tiny little claws? I'll tell you, Joan, a cat can do *lots* of damage. It can blind a dog, for sure. Kill it, maybe, if it catches it right." She cocked her head. "So why don't you just think of me as a cat." She cocked her head the other way and nodded at the knife she still held in front of her eyes. "And this," she said, "is my claw."

* * *

The world Ryerson was seeing was a world no human eyes had ever seen before. It was a black and white world whose focus shifted from moment to moment as the creature viewing it gauged where a threat lay and where food could be had. At the moment those were the creature's primary concerns. It was also trying to take the measure of the man who had invaded its territory, trying to determine if the man was going to close in on its nest, or if the man was going to fall over—as some of them did—and so make a kind of offering of himself.

And because the creature's concerns included the man, the world Ryerson was seeing included—from random moment to random moment—himself. His tweed sport coat, his corduroy slacks, his Wallabees. And his fear. The rigid set of his jaw, the stiffness of his limbs. Fear that he would not make it back to the car in time. Fear that he would again become blind because the creature whose eyes he was using would run off in search of something more interesting.

So Ryerson began to commit to memory all that he was seeing through the eyes of the creature watching him—the doorway a few feet to his right (it had the word "DELIVERY" over it), the wall behind him, the broad expanse of the curb in front of him. Then the creature's gaze shifted and he saw the street like a mouth yawning wide, and the great gray walls of the buildings.

The creature's gaze shifted quickly about. Ryerson saw windows high on the wall above him; to the east, the heavily chromed front end of the Woody, parked a hundred feet away; beyond it, the suggestion of movement, as of someone moving on the street. Then he saw himself; he saw his fear again. And he felt, as well, the sudden and overwhelming onslaught of a much more primal kind of fear from the creature whose eyes he was using.

And a flash of matted fur fell into that creature's line of vision; a great gaping mouth and huge almond-shaped eyes appeared, and the creature's gaze steadied for just an instant on that mouth and those eyes. Then it bolted. But too late. The black and white geometry of its world faded and was gone.

And Ryerson, having committed to memory exactly what he had seen through that poor damned creature's eyes, set off blindly toward the Woody.

Doreen moved in her graceful and deliberate way into Joan's bedroom, brandishing the small silver knife ahead of her.

Joan sat very still on the bed. She whispered, "I don't *know* you, I don't *know* you!"

And Doreen said again, "Of course you don't. But *I* know you."

Joan shook her head. "Please don't hurt me."

Doreen continued advancing very slowly

The Devouring

and deliberately on her. "Hurtin's what I was made to do, honey. It's what we were all made to do. It's what we have to do, or we don't do nothin' no more," she said, and took an amazingly quick swing with the knife and opened a long thin wound across the top of Joan's chest, just above her blue nightgown. The wound seeped blood at once. Joan gasped, put her hand to the wound, looked at her fingers, saw the blood there, and looked in awe at Doreen. "But I don't *know* you, I *don't* know you," she pleaded, her voice a breathy, incredulous whisper.

And Doreen said, "You don't really believe that anymore, do ya, honey? I think you know who I am. I think you *want* me to cut you up." She grinned a wide grin of amusement and expectation. "And you know what? That's exactly what I'm gonna do." She took another swing. Joan tried to back away from it, but too late. The knife sank an inch into her chest just below the first wound. Joan reeled backward, across the bed, hand clutching the new wound. "No," she screeched, "please, no!"

Doreen cooed, "I got to, Joan. I really got to." And she lunged.

Chapter Twenty-Three

Near the Buffalo city limits, as Ryerson pushed the Woody to its top speed of fifty, a patrol car pulled out of a side street, paced him a few moments, flashed its lights at him, then gave him a blast on its siren. Ryerson kept going. He was less than two minutes away from Joan's house; if necessary, he thought he could keep the cop behind him until then.

The patrol car's roof lights came on, followed by another shrill blast of the siren, then the car swerved hard into the left-hand lane and Ryerson heard faintly, beneath the clatter of the Woody's engine, "Pull over immediately!"

Ryerson switched on his interior lights and turned his head toward the patrol car. "Emergency!" he mouthed at it.

"Pull over immediately!" he heard again.

He pointed urgently ahead. "Emergency!" he mouthed once more. "E-mer-gen-cy!"

And he heard at once, "I'll follow you!"

They pulled into the driveway. Ryerson jumped from the Woody and ran across the lawn toward the house, the cop close behind him, their way illuminated by the spotlight over the garage. And as Ryerson ran, he wept. As he pushed himself through the litter of evil around him, as he swept his arms wide in a futile effort to sweep away the demons that crowded the lawn like weeds and wrapped themselves around his legs and leaped ineffectually upon his back and hunkered about on scrawny thighs and laughed and giggled and moaned, he wept.

These were creatures which—like the slime left behind by snails—had been left in the wake of the evil thing that had visited this house.

"Wait there, please!" the cop behind Ryerson called.

Ryerson waved violently in the air.

"Wait there!" the cop repeated.

"No," Ryerson screamed. "Dammit, no!" And he ran through the debris of evil, arms swinging, feet kicking out occasionally, and futilely, to the porch. He threw the door open.

He did not go inside.

He knew only too well what he would find there.

In the Records Division

"There's one thing you could try," Glen said. "I mean, if you really want a look in that locker."

"Yes," Irene said, "I do."

"Simple," he said, and smiled.

"Yes, yes, go on. Do I link up this computer with the Greyhound computer, search out the hard disk subsystem? What?"

"No, Irene. You get a set of master keys and you go and open the locker up."

She was aghast. "I couldn't do that. What if someone caught me?"

"Then you'd be in a lot of trouble. But it's probably the only way you're going to be able to get into that locker. And if you're right about Lucas, if he really does want to be caught, then he'd probably welcome it."

Irene looked blankly at him a few moments, then she sputtered, "Wh-where do I get a set of master keys?"

Glen opened the top drawer of his desk and made a show of peering in. "It just so happens ..." He looked up, grinned. "They're not free, Irene. I mean, I've got 'em just for the night, until Detective Triano comes in, so they're not free."

She sighed. "Okay, okay, name your price."

"Dinner and a movie. That's pretty cheap, I'd say."

She nodded. "Sure. Okay."

"Smart girl." He reached into the drawer,

took out a set of perhaps 100 keys of various types—all on a huge key ring—and tossed them to her. "Friday evening," he said. "I know it'll be an evening to remember."

Ryerson kneeled over what was left of Joan Mott Evans. Her body lay on its back on the bed, arms wide, legs together, as if she were on some invisible cross. And the green nightgown she wore was streaked everywhere with her blood.

Behind him, in the bedroom doorway, the cop breathed, "Jee-sus H. Christ!"

Ryerson, his gaze on Joan's open eyes, waved at him to go away. "Leave us alone," he pleaded.

"I sure as hell will not . . ."

Ryerson reeled around, his face a mask of agony. "For the love of God, let me say good-bye to her."

The cop hesitated.

Ryerson hurried on. "I won't touch anything. Just, please, let me be alone with her."

The cop said nothing for a few moments. Then, "Sure, pal. Just, like you said, don't touch nothin'. Not her, not nothin'! You understand what I'm saying to you?"

"Yes," Ryerson nodded. "Thank you."

The cop sighed, glanced around the room, then looked at Ryerson again. "Is the phone in the kitchen?"

"No," Ryerson managed, voice trembling. "It's in the living room. It's on an end table."

The cop nodded at Joan. "She your wife?"
"No. A friend."
"Sure," the cop said. "I understand." He gestured toward the living room. "I'll be phoning this in. You got five minutes." A short pause. "Oh, leave the door open, okay?" And he disappeared into the living room.

Ryerson turned back to Joan. He shook his head briskly in disbelief. He whispered, "Why, Joan? My God, why?"

She lay very still.

His eyes scanned the wounds that traced her body like a hundred dark red tattoos; they crisscrossed here, paralleled there, formed a rough circle there, there a rough triangle, there what could have been the letter *C*, there what looked like the number two. Some of the wounds had let copious amounts of blood, but most were all but dry, and this told Ryerson that thankfully, she had died early in the attack.

Grief was, strangely, a new experience for him. He'd never lost anyone terribly close, except his mother, who had died when he was not yet into his teens. What grief he'd felt since then had been the grief of others—a friend whose father died in an automobile accident, a business acquaintance whose wife died of leukemia. And although their grief bore into him, although there had been moments when he felt their grief almost as strongly as they did, for a quarter of a century he had never faced the prospect of living with grief interminably.

That prospect hit him very hard now. It made him numb and speechless; it made him want to crawl into himself and hide from the obscenity that had happened here.

And it was that need, that compulsion to run from his grief, that nearly made him deaf to her.

Nearly made her words—which vaulted the ever-widening gap between death and life—inaudible.

But even through his grief he heard her, and he said aloud, "Joan?"

Her body did not respond. Her eyes were fixed, her pupils dilated, her heart quiet, her blood was rapidly congealing in her veins. But still she spoke to him. And because she was beyond the limitations that life imposes, she told him many things at once. And he heard them all.

She told him how much she loved him. How much she longed to be with him. How precious their brief time together had been, that she would carry that time with her through eternity. That she had real happiness now, and peace.

And at last she told him that she knew her murderer. She told him, too, that although she knew better now—and he even heard a wry chuckle from her at that—in life she would have said that her murder was just.

And then she was gone.

Ryerson stepped away from the body on the bed. All at once he did not see it as Joan Mott Evans. He saw it as the home where her spirit had lived for a few years. And now her spirit had flown from it.

His gaze lifted and passed slowly about the room. He saw that the debris that littered the lawn and pranced about droolingly in the other rooms and hung from the windows and hunkered around on greasy thighs was nowhere in evidence here.

He said aloud, his voice still trembling, but as much now with hope as with grief, "Good-bye, Joan."

He went into the living room. The cop was there, notepad in hand, one wide-mouthed, gauzy-eyed, translucent demon hanging around his neck; another, a dull burnt orange, was shimmying up his leg on incredibly long, thin arms. The cop nodded toward the bedroom. "You finished?"

Ryerson nodded.

"Are you up to answering a few questions then?"

"Sure," Ryerson answered, and gestured to indicate a short hallway off the living room. "Bathroom first," he said.

The cop shook his head. "I can't let you go in there. I'm sorry. If I let you corrupt the crime scene—" He stopped. "Whatcha gotta do? Take a leak?"

Ryerson nodded.

"Okay, then. But like I said before, don't touch nothin'."

Ryerson started for the bathroom; the cop called after him. "Flush it with your elbow, okay, buddy?"

"Yes, okay," Ryerson said.

"And if you—" He stopped, apparently unsure of himself. He continued. "I'm sorry, but if you ... find anything—in the toilet, I mean—let me know before you use it."

"You're very thorough," Ryerson said.

"Sure," the cop said, as if aware he was being humored, and Ryerson went down the hallway to the bathroom.

The cop knocked on the door half a minute later. "Hey, buddy," he called, "on second thought, why don't you go out back or something, okay?"

There was no response. He knocked again. "You hear me, buddy?"

Still nothing. He pushed the door open.

The bathroom was empty.

"Dammit!" Ryerson breathed as the Woody clattered to life. Beneath that clatter he could hear the wail of sirens to the east; he hoped the grisly trail he'd be following did not lead in their direction.

He put the Woody in gear, glanced to his left at the front door of the house, saw the cop appear there and unholster his weapon. He put the accelerator pedal to the floor; the Woody ambled backward and hit the patrol car just behind it with a thud. He desperately put it in first, pulled forward, glanced to his left again. The cop had the gun leveled at him and had assumed a wide-legged, straight-armed stance. "I don't wanta shoot you!" he screeched. Ryerson caught and held the man's gaze. He realized that he was telling the truth—he did indeed not want to shoot, and the chances were only slight that he would. Ryerson put the Woody in reverse, and backed around the patrol car while the cop, maintaining his military stance all the while, duck-walked in a half circle to keep Ryerson in his sights.

Ryerson backed out of the driveway and swung the Woody around so it was facing east. He could see a soft, undulating red glow at the end of the street, beyond the glare of the high beams. But in the light of the high beams themselves, he saw only the street. And that meant that the evil thing that had visited Joan's house had gone in some other direction. He pulled quickly back into the driveway, noted that the cop was still keeping him in his sights. He yelled through the open window at the cop, "Call Captain Lucas. Tell him to meet Ryerson Biergarten at Frank's Place. He knows where it is."

The cop yelled back, "Get out of the car!" and cocked the gun.

Ryerson kept his eyes on him. He realized that the chances were now about fifty-fifty that the cop would fire. "And if you can't get hold of Captain Lucas," he yelled, aware that the wail of sirens was very close now, that he had perhaps thirty seconds before the other cars arrived, "call Guy Mallory and tell him the same thing." And he put the Woody in reverse, backed out of the driveway again, and swung around so he was facing west.

His high beams showed him what he had expected to see—the obscene debris left in the wake of the thing that had visited here lay at random on the street in a kind of zigzagging trail. He floored the accelerator. With aching slowness the Woody clattered off to the west, but not before a bullet tore through the passenger window, then through the windshield, which exploded in a shower of shattered glass. Ryerson felt a dozen or more wounds open on his face and arms.

Chapter Twenty-Four

What did duty mean? Jack Lucas wanted to know. And how had he so easily and quickly given it up? Was he really, as Doreen had called him, "just 240 pounds of groin and cowardice"? Yes, he was. She'd proven it.

Because, for God's sake, what had she done except give herself to him and then threaten to take it all away? Other women had done the same thing. His first wife had. His girlfriend Monica had, and they'd fought it out and then had continued seeing each other, although with the understanding that he would call the shots, not her, that he would say when and how and where—and that's as it was intended to be, right? Sure, the relationship had ended in time. But everything ends. Even the bad things end. You win a few, you lose a few.

And hadn't he thought that he'd won very,

very big with Doreen? Hadn't the ecstasy he'd known with her been beyond anything he might have imagined? And hadn't she proved that he was indeed "just 240 pounds of groin and cowardice"? *Here it is, Bozo; taste it, touch it, play with it. That's a good boy. Now, if you stop being a good boy, I'm going to take all these wonderful toys away from you.*

He wasn't forty-five years old. He was fourteen and he had his hand on a bare tit for the first time and his cock was rising and his heart was pumping hard and fast and his mouth was watering because he'd discovered what life was really all about.

But Doreen had nothing to do with life. He'd known that almost from the beginning. She had nothing at all to do with life.

He did. And that was the key, he realized at last, to the power she had over him.

The key to the power she had over everyone in that place.

Finally he understood what she had meant when she'd told him, "I am the link between death and life, between the living and the dead. I can show you what lies inside you—your power, your immortality."

He swung the big Mercury Grand Marquis tight around the corner onto Peacock Street.

Irene caught the eye of the burly Greyhound Package Express attendant, smiled, and decided to take a chance. He was halfway across the big, dark room, behind a waist-high counter. She pulled her shield from a vest pocket, flashed it at him, said loudly, "Police business," and nodded toward the bank of lockers in front of her.

He looked at her a moment, then at the lockers, then shrugged and disappeared into the baggage area.

Irene hurried over to the lockers. She found locker number 843—the second of the three numbers that had appeared on her monitor—and began to insert keys in the lock.

Ryerson was not quite a mile from Joan's house, on a long, straight stretch of road bordered on both sides by several hundred flat and empty acres (soon to be the home of an industrial park—a kind of halfway zone between the city and the suburbs), when a pulsating red light appeared far behind him.

In the glare of his own lights he could see that the grisly trail he was following was growing thinner—there an owl-eyed, bloated thing writhing at the side of the road, a hundred feet beyond it, something long and thin and sickeningly translucent smashed flat against the pavement, and a good distance beyond that, something bright pink, big-knuckled and fanged, hopped about on huge, flat human feet.

And when he looked in the rearview mirror, he saw that the car was advancing very quickly on him, that he had maybe another twenty or thirty seconds until it pulled alongside and he'd have no choice but to stop.

He sighed. It had been a desperate idea anyway—the idea that what was left in the wake of the evil thing that had murdered Joan would lead him to it, and so to his confrontation with it.

He longed for that confrontation.

If only for his own peace of mind.

Now, he thought, that confrontation was going to be postponed.

He sighed again; he felt his eyes water, felt a cold flower of grief and loneliness and fear blossom in his stomach.

And he pulled the Woody over to the curb and waited for what he supposed was a patrol car to catch up with him.

Benny Bloom felt the change starting. It always started the same way. His insides felt as if they were solidifying, as if someone else were trying to shoulder in to the space he inhabited. And then—like Laurie Drake, Lilian Janus, Andrew Spurling, and a half-dozen others—he had watched himself do things that were murderous and obscene, things that made him cringe and chuckle and weep and laugh all at the same time.

Because it was all Benny Bloom.

And the form—changed or not—didn't matter a bit.

It was all Benny Bloom. Just as it had all

been Lilian Janus, Andrew Spurling, Laurie Drake, Leonard McGuire.

"I am the link between death and life," she had told him. "Between the living and the dead. I can show you what lives inside you and makes you immortal, the children you produce within yourself—the children of your desires and your needs and fantasies."

He had believed her. They all had.

That's why they were dying here. In this big, damp room.

Because this was her feeding station.

This was where she took their power from them and absorbed it and left them to languish and die.

Benny fought the change as it began. He clung to the idea he had of himself, of the Benny who was a wimp and a nerd, the Benny whose only friends were other wimps and nerds, the Benny who hurt no one but himself.

And because he fought the change—just as Laurie Drake and Leonard McGuire, and Andrew Spurling had—it fought him, and it brought him incredible pain, because the entity struggling within him, the child of his desires and fantasies, was creating itself.

Irene Sabitch whispered, "It never happens this way. The *last* key is always the one that works." She'd inserted only a dozen or so keys into the lock, and the locker had opened.

A manila envelope lay anticlimactically within. She had expected much more. She wasn't sure how much more—files, computer disks, wads of money perhaps. But much more than this lone manila envelope.

She hesitated, glanced nervously around. The Package Express attendant was again behind the counter, attention on a magazine. She looked back at the manila envelope, inhaled, as if to give herself strength, and picked it up. She didn't open it at once. She tried to gauge its contents by touch first, and as she did, her brow furrowed in confusion. She spread the mouth of the envelope, looked in. "My God," she whispered, "*cock*tail napkins!"

Ryerson did not turn off the Woody's engine or headlights. The lights were necessary to him; he did not want to become blind here, did not want his only link to the world around him to be the pulsating red light in the rearview mirror as it grew closer, and brighter, and more urgent.

Resignedly, he began to study the pattern of wounds on his hands, where small fragments of the windshield had sliced into him. He thought how very much like some of Joan's wounds they were, and as that thought came to him, another cold flower of grief and loneliness blossomed inside him and he began to weep—not for Joan, but for himself.

He lowered his head as he wept. When he

raised it, because the wail of the siren behind him had stopped, he saw Doreen grinning at him through the space where the windshield had been.

He screamed. It was a hard and deafening roar—a scream of sudden fear.

Doreen's grin became a leer. She said to him, "Your lady friend ain't gonna do *you* no favors anymore. You got Do*reen* for that now!"

He couldn't help it. Grief and anger moved him. With a speed born of desperation, he grabbed Doreen by the throat and squeezed very hard, so the wounds on the backs of his hands spurted blood.

Doreen continued to grin. "Whatchoo doin', Mr. Biergarten?" she said, her words soft and amused. "You can't kill me. I'm gonna show you what *livin's* all about."

He pushed at her—his intention was to send her reeling backward. But it was like pushing at a tree. His own body went back hard into the seat. And still grinning, voluptuous, deadly, she stayed precisely where she was—leaning into the space where the windshield had been.

She said, "You're a joke, my man. You think you got power?"

His mouth moved a little, but nothing coherent came from it. Doreen's face was awash now in the glare of the headlights of the approaching car. Her grin altered. "And sure you got power, you just don't know what kinda power you got. I been on the other side, man. I got death in here." Her hands went to her breasts, cupped them. "So I *know* what power is."

Ryerson became aware that the car behind him was coming to a halt.

Doreen cooed on. "I got death all around me, Mr. Biergarten. I got death for insides. Where other people got a heart and lungs and stomach, I got death. *She* gave that to me. Joan gave that to me."

Ryerson whispered, "You're Lila Curtis."

Doreen shrugged. "I don't know any Lila Curtis no more. I used to. I used to live inside her. An' then she lived inside me. For a while, anyway. Till your little girlfriend put a bullet into her. Now there's just me. And I got death inside me, so I *know* what power is. *Life* is power, my man! *Life* is power! And I've been awful hungry lately."

The first bullets tore through the back window of the Woody, and zipped past the side of Ryerson's head. A hole appeared at the left side of Doreen's forehead. It looked like a hole in an overripe apple. She grinned again, as if she were being caressed. "You all got *life*, Mr. Biergarten. So you all got *power*! Why don't you just give a little bit of it to Doreen?" And she lunged at him through the space where the windshield had been.

Ryerson threw his door open, launched himself from the car, tucked, rolled, and came to a stop ten feet away, on the shoulder of the road, in tall grass. He lay on his stomach, with his arms beneath him and a tremendous pain coursing through his shoulder.

He looked back at the Woody.

"For the love of God," he whispered.

Doreen was on her stomach, head and torso out the door of the car, her legs on the seat, and her arms back so her chin and breasts were on the pavement. She stared at him, her eyes as big and opaque as walnuts. She grinned; that hideous wound at her forehead oozed a whitish buttery substance. And she twitched as if with periodic and random pulses of electricity, as if she were some kind of high school biology experiment.

And the man standing over her with his .38 aimed at her head looked quizzically at Ryerson, then back at Doreen, then at Ryerson again. "What's this?" he said. He looked back at Doreen and said, as if to himself, "What's this? It stinks!" and he slowly and systematically unloaded the .38 into Doreen's head. On the sixth shot it shattered and all the stuff that filled it up drained from inside it and began to collect into a little pool where the road dipped at the curb.

Chapter Twenty-Five

It's been said that there's as much water in the world today as there was a hundred million years ago. Only its form changes. It freezes. It vaporizes. It flows. So time means nothing to it. It changes according to the environment. And for these past one hundred million years, the creatures that have lived on the planet have variously been kept alive by it, drowned in it, swept away by it. The water that rises as a vapor from the Caspian Sea may find its way years later to a lake in the Adirondacks. It knows nothing, of course, of those years it spent floating about in the upper atmosphere. It does what the environment tells it to do. And it never goes away.

Irene Sabitch scowled. A dozen cocktail napkins, each with no more than a name on it—"George," "Sam," "Tanya," "Melanie,"

"Scott," "Miles"; each written in black ink in big block letters. She flipped through the dozen napkins, stuffed them into the manila envelope, and put the envelope back into the locker. *And for this*, she thought, *I've got to spend an evening with Glen Coffman*. She stalked from the Greyhound Package Express office to her car. She whispered, as she turned the ignition on, "There's no damned justice in the world, no damned justice at all."

Jack Lucas took a very long time redirecting the aim of his .38 from what was left of Doreen to his temple. Suicide was anathema to him. A close friend in college had committed suicide and he—Jack Lucas—had spent a full year in anguish over it, trying, futilely, to square it with his view of life, a view that said that since he could not create life, he had no right to take life. Not even his own.

But of course that noble philosophy had been tossed upon the dungheap of recent events. He remembered with grisly clarity the faces of each of the dozen or more transients he had picked up in "The District" in the last five months.

Since he'd come back from Erie.

Since he'd brought this thing that lay at his feet back with him from Erie. So it could feed on the life he brought her, and so eventually find life for itself.

And, at last, so it could seek out the

woman who had brought her so much torment. Joan Mott Evans. And do with her what it pleased.

He remembered all the sad, hopeful, rheumy-eyed faces of the men he had sent into that bar.

He remembered, too, the faces of the bright and vibrant young people he had brought to her.

And the ones she had found for herself. Like Laurie Drake, Leonard McGuire, Lilian Janus. And the others.

He knew that those faces would be with him forever.

He turned his head very slowly toward Ryerson, the barrel of the .38 still pointed at his temple. In an area of his brain detached from the urgency of the moment, from what he saw as the justice of his own suicide, an idea was forming. It was an idea he could not verbalize because it moved away from his grasp when he tried to touch it and examine it. It was much like the vision that had come to Ryerson the day before, when his mind's eye had shown him a hive of workers and drones all working in attendance to the queen bee. Except now the queen had been removed from the hive. And the hive was not a hive at all; and the workers and drones were not bees. They were human.

"Don't do it," Ryerson called. Trying to ignore the agonizing pain in his shoulder, he pushed himself to his feet and started across the road toward Lucas.

Not bees, but human beings laboring furiously in attendance to a huge and evil queen so it could grow fat and powerful and could seek out life for itself.

"Don't do it, please don't do it!" Ryerson screamed.

"We do what we have to do," Jack Lucas said.

Ryerson grabbed his arm tightly against the throbbing pain.

Lucas went on. "She told me she could give me life; she told me she could give me immortality. All I had to do was . . . be someone else. Simple, huh?"

"Put the gun down, Captain Lucas. Please put the gun down."

Lucas said nothing.

"There's so much work to do," Ryerson said; he didn't know where the phrase had come from—perhaps from some need that had vaulted from Lucas to him.

Lucas nodded slowly. "Yes," he said. "Work to be done." Then he lowered his .38 and fell sobbing to his knees.

Epilogue

A Week Later

What in life gets resolved? Ryerson wondered. Very little, really. The memories linger, although they're often incomplete, or they're a litany of mistakes, or they're memories of happiness brought to an abrupt and awful end.

Like his time with Joan.

He pulled the Volkswagen Beetle onto Bailey Avenue. It would lead him east, to Route 33, to Interstate 90, then to Rochester, where he planned to stop and see his friend, Chief of Detectives Tom McCabe. He was much in need of friendship just now.

He reached across the seat and stroked the sleeping Creosote. "We'll find out what's wrong with you, boy," he said, because Dr. Craig Gibson, D.V.M., had, after a lengthy series of tests, been able to proclaim only, "He's allergic to something. Don't ask me what." Then he'd smiled. "Maybe he's allergic to those demons you've been harping about all week, Mr. Biergarten."

Ryerson hoped the Volkswagen possessed the same kind of happy memories that the Woody had, before Doreen had corrupted it. When his mind cleared, and his psyche got back into focus, he'd find out.

He came to a stop at a red light, heard a motorcycle pull up next to him, and glanced over at it. He saw that a woman of sixty was astride it, her leathers polished, her mouth drawn into a huge smile. Ryerson thought, "She's happy! She's herself."

The light changed. The woman goosed the accelerator of the big Harley and roared off. Ryerson touched the Beetle's accelerator so it tiptoed cautiously through the intersection.

Then, because of all that he had learned in the past two weeks about love, death, grief, and hope, he said, "Good-bye, Joan. I'll see you in a while," and steered the Beetle toward Route 33.

Ramsey Campbell

☐ 51652-4	DARK COMPANIONS		$3.50
51653-2		Canada	$3.95
☐ 51654-0	THE DOLL WHO ATE HIS		$3.50
51655-9	MOTHER	Canada	$3.95
☐ 51658-3	THE FACE THAT MUST DIE		$3.95
51659-1		Canada	$4.95
☐ 51650-8	INCARNATE		$3.95
51651-6		Canada	$4.50
☐ 58125-3	THE NAMELESS		$3.50
58126-1		Canada	$3.95
☐ 51656-7	OBSESSION		$3.95
51657-5		Canada	$4.95

Buy them at your local bookstore or use this handy coupon:
Clip and mail this page with your order

TOR BOOKS—Reader Service Dept.
49 W. 24 Street, 9th Floor, New York, NY 10010

Please send me the book(s) I have checked above. I am enclosing $_____ (please add $1.00 to cover postage and handling). Send check or money order only—no cash or C.O.D.'s.

Mr./Mrs./Miss _____
Address _____
City _____ State/Zip _____
Please allow six weeks for delivery. Prices subject to change without notice.

JOHN FARRIS

"America's premier novelist of terror. When he turns it on, nobody does it better." —Stephen King

"Farris is a giant of contemporary horror!"
—Peter Straub

☐	58264-0	ALL HEADS TURN WHEN	$3.50
	58265-9	THE HUNT GOES BY	Canada $4.50
☐	58260-8	THE CAPTORS	$3.50
	58261-6		Canada $3.95
☐	58262-4	THE FURY	$3.50
	58263-2		Canada $4.50
☐	58258-6	MINOTAUR	$3.95
	58259-4		Canada $4.95
☐	58266-7	SON OF THE ENDLESS NIGHT	$4.50
	58267-5		Canada $5.50
☐	58268-3	SHATTER	$3.50
	58269-1		Canada $4.50
☐	58270-5	WILDWOOD	$4.50
	58271-3		Canada $5.95

AVAILABLE IN JANUARY
☐	58272-1	CATACOMBS	$3.95
	58273-X		Canada $4.95

Buy them at your local bookstore or use this handy coupon:
Clip and mail this page with your order

TOR BOOKS—Reader Service Dept.
49 West 24 Street, 9th Floor, New York, N.Y. 10010

Please send me the book(s) I have checked above. I am enclosing
$_____ (please add $1.00 to cover postage and handling).
Send check or money order only—no cash or C.O.D.'s.

Mr./Mrs./Miss _____
Address _____
City _____ State/Zip _____
Please allow six weeks for delivery. Prices subject to change without notice.

GRAHAM MASTERTON

- [ ] 52195-1 CONDOR $3.50
  52196-X Canada $3.95

- [ ] 52191-9 IKON $3.95
  52192-7 Canada $4.50

- [ ] 52193-5 THE PARIAH $3.50
  52194-3 Canada $3.95

- [ ] 52189-7 SOLITAIRE $3.95
  52190-0 Canada $4.50

- [ ] 48067-9 THE SPHINX $2.95

- [ ] 48061-X TENGU $3.50

- [ ] 48042-3 THE WELLS OF HELL $2.95

- [ ] 52199-4 PICTURE OF EVIL $3.95
  52200-1 Canada $4.95

Buy them at your local bookstore or use this handy coupon:
Clip and mail this page with your order

TOR BOOKS—Reader Service Dept.
49 W. 24 Street, 9th Floor, New York, NY 10010

Please send me the book(s) I have checked above. I am enclosing $_____ (please add $1.00 to cover postage and handling). Send check or money order only—no cash or C.O.D.'s.

Mr./Mrs./Miss _____
Address _____
City _____ State/Zip _____
Please allow six weeks for delivery. Prices subject to change without notice.

THE BEST IN HORROR

- [ ] 58270-5　WILDWOOD by John Farris　　　　$4.50
　　　58271-3　　　　　　　　　　　　　　Canada $5.95
- [ ] 52760-7　THE WAITING ROOM　　　　　　$3.95
　　　52761-5　by T. M. Wright　　　　　　Canada $4.95
- [ ] 51762-8　MASTERS OF DARKNESS edited　　3.95
　　　51763-6　by Dennis Etchinson　　　　Canada $4.95
- [ ] 52623-6　BLOOD HERITAGE　　　　　　　$3.50
　　　52624-4　by Sheri S. Tepper　　　　Canada $4.50
- [ ] 50070-9　THE NIGHT OF THE RIPPER　　　$3.50
　　　50071-7　by Robert Bloch　　　　　　Canada $4.50
- [ ] 52558-2　TOTENTANZ by Al Sarrantonio　　$3.50
　　　52559-0　　　　　　　　　　　　　　Canada $4.50
- [ ] 58226-8　WHEN DARKNESS LOVES US　　　$3.50
　　　58227-6　by Elizabeth Engstrom　　　Canada $4.50
- [ ] 51656-7　OBSESSION by Ramsey Campbell　$3.95
　　　51657-5　　　　　　　　　　　　　　Canada $4.95
- [ ] 51850-0　MIDNIGHT edited by　　　　　　$2.95
　　　51851-9　Charles L. Grant　　　　　　Canada $3.50
- [ ] 52445-4　KACHINA by Kathryn Ptacek　　　$3.95
　　　52446-2　　　　　　　　　　　　　　Canada $4.95
- [ ] 52541-8　DEAD WHITE by Alan Ryan　　　$3.50
　　　52542-6　　　　　　　　　　　　　　Canada $3.95

Buy them at your local bookstore or use this handy coupon:
Clip and mail this page with your order

TOR BOOKS—Reader Service Dept.
49 W. 24 Street, 9th Floor, New York, NY 10010

Please send me the book(s) I have checked above. I am enclosing $_____ (please add $1.00 to cover postage and handling). Send check or money order only—no cash or C.O.D.'s.

Mr./Mrs./Miss _____
Address _____
City _____ State/Zip _____

Please allow six weeks for delivery. Prices subject to change without notice.